YOUR FAITH WILL SUSTAIN YOU, AND YOU WILL PREVAIL

The Life Story of Jacob and Elisabeth Isaak

Drs. Helmut Isaak

TRANSLATION:
Dr. Jack Thiessen 2014

EDITING AND PROOF-READING:
Helmut and Eva Isaak

Cover Design and Typesetting:
Caitlin Voth

Translation:
Dr. Jack Thiessen

Editing:
Helmut and Eva Isaak

Cover Photograph:
Jacob and Elisabeth Isaak
in front of the Mennonite
Church

The Life Story of Jacob
and Elisabeth Isaak as
told by their children and
grandchildren.

If you lose your faith, you will fail
(Isaiah 7:9).

Impressum:
Herausgeber: Verlagsagentur Rudolf Dück Sawatzky
25451 Quickborn, Deutschland

Verfasser: Helmut Isaak, Kanada.

Herstellung und Verlag
BoD - Books on Demand, Norderstedt

9 783735 757685

TABLE OF CONTENTS

FOREWORD

THE STORY, and thus the history of Jacob and Elisabeth Isaak started in Russia.

Their childhood, the Czar Era, then Communism, followed by the Reign of Terror, Suppression and Persecution, the constant fear of falling victim to the Red Terror; they then decide to leave everything behind and travel to Moscow. Once there, together with many thousands of like-minded refugees, they apply for permission to leave and, in time, are bound for Paraguay.

In the Chaco a new home was built, attended by countless challenges and tests, but also blessings.

This story was documented by Helmut Isaak in cooperation with his siblings. It describes the life of two people who fought the mighty battle of life itself; a battle which pushed them to their very limits, during which they bowed to no one except God: Jacob and Elisabeth (nee Hildebrandt) Isaak.

While Elisabeth, together with the eleven children looked after the home and also their farm, Jacob was fully involved in the services for his society, for the congregation, and for God. As a result of this multifold endeavor, they enriched the lives of many who walked a common path towards a common aim. Furthermore this commitment was obviously blessed richly from, and by, Eternal Sources for the benefit of all.

For Jacob and Elisabeth Isaak the departure for Moscow, the continuing journey to Paraguay via Germany, and the life and service among as well as for their fellow believers in the Chaco was, above all, a central, indeed vital issue, of faith and obedience.

This memoire embedded in the monumental events of the twentieth century is here depicted by Helmut Isaak in true to life, suspenseful story and in a language both readily accessible and compelling.

The life of these two people was not borne by fate or destiny, but by God's guidance and direction. They were indeed guided by the Divine maxim: Your faith will sustain you, and you will prevail.

Uwe Friesen
Chairman of
The Society for Mennonite
History and Culture
in Paraguay

INTRODUCTION

THE MATERIAL FOR THE STORY and history of our parents Jacob and Elisabeth Isaak was compiled over many years. Important sources to that end were located and gathered in and from Russia, Germany, Paraguay and Canada. Many personal interviews were conducted with contemporaries of our parents. Children and grandchildren were questioned; they have all contributed to the contents of this book. One name deserving of special mention is Gisela Isaak Voth, my daughter, who helped me with the interviews in Paraguay in 2010.

The main source for father's theological world of ideas were his sermons, his numerous talks and papers presented, which he wrote out in detail or left behind in fragments, coded or in scripted detail.

This book makes no claim to being an academic biography. If that were the intent, then all the minutes and protocols of church meetings would have to be researched, including those of church and mission committees which are housed in the various archives in Filadelfia. Researching his extensive correspondence with the MCC and representatives of the General Conference, would necessitate trips to Winnipeg, Akron, Goshen and Newton, to name only a few of the many archives.

This history of our parents is an excerpt from their lives and is intended for life and lives itself, for that matter. Moreover, it is meant to be a testimony to their faith. By their faith and obedience they, and their fellow believers, with all representing the

Chaco pioneers, who, through hard work, were able to transform the primeval lands into the promised land of milk and honey, particularly if sufficient rain fell and in good time.

The gathering of this material, as well as the compilation of this book, amounted to a rich blessing for me, the author.

Helmut Isaak

CHAPTER I

Your Faith Will Sustain You, and You Will Prevail

AT THE OCCASION of the Golden Wedding Anniversary of Jacob and Elisabeth Isaak, Isaiah 7:9 was chosen by one of the sons, Helmut, as the motto for his parent's life; he then interpreted this portion of scripture.

These words were communicated by God through the prophet Isaiah to King Ahas when Jerusalem was surrounded by enemies of military superiority:The future of the people of Israel in general does not depend as much on the strength of its military or the formidable walls of Jerusalem, as it does in the faith and confidence in the divine plan of salvation.

God has constantly involved Himself in the history of His people, when it came to be or not to be. When the Hebrews fled Egypt and the reigning pharaoh surrounded the Israelites by the Red Sea, God had Moses speak to His people as follows: And Moses said unto the people,

> Do not be afraid. Stand firm and you will see the deliverance the Lord will bring you today. The Egyptians you see today you will never see again. The Lord will fight for you; you need only to be still (Exodus 14: 13-14).

The Golden Wedding Anniversary of our parents with the family.

Your faith will sustain you, and you will prevail. If you lack faith, you will fail. In other words, the future of the people of God, depends exclusively on their faith. Faith for Israel means that it accepts, in childlike confidence and obedience, the course of God's salvation.

"Your faith will sustain you, and you will prevail" also applies to the New Testament. The existence, duration and the future of the church of Jesus Christ, the new people of God depends on their faith and confidence in God's promises.

For Jacob and Elisabeth Isaak the departure for Moscow, the trip through Germany, and then on to Paraguay was indeed a matter of faith and obedience. To them, and for them, the guiding motto: Your faith will sustain you, and you will prevail, applied then as now.

AUGUST 1930: FROM THE AUHAGEN ESTATE INTO THE CHACO BUSH

The former inhabitants of the Auhagen villagers named their first tent camp in the Chaco Settlement an Estate as well, obviously with a serious dash of irony in their humor.

Evening has again settled upon us. All the camp fires have been extinguished. It is black night. A cold dry wind is blowing from the south. Over the canvases of the vast tent expanse, the Chaco sky, a sky of a clarity heretofore never witnessed by any of the recently arrived Auhagen settlers, covers all. Occasionally the barking of a nosing fox or the crying of a needy child is to be heard. The adult population is restlessly seeking for that comfortable spot on their hard straw beds. Too much has transpired over the last few years, months, weeks and days for them to find the tranquility of needed rest. Very much has transpired, and now this load of experience needs coming to terms with emotionally. First, there was the departure for Moscow, where thousands of Germans, Mennonites, Catholics and Evangelicals gathered in the hope of departing for Germany. Then came the desperate wait, the wait of uncertainty. The nights in the Moscow suburbs were invariably pregnant with the suspense of Angst.

Will the Black Raven of the GPU (Secret Police) descend upon them at midnight to arrest a father, brother or uncle and take him away, never to be seen again; such fear was a constant. Then the miracle occurred. Some 6,000 refugees received permission to leave for freedom. However, they lack the passports of citizenship, and so Canada or the USA, which was their desired destinations, rejected them out of hand, and so they arrived, in time, in the Green Hell of the Paraguayan Chaco Bush.

During the Romanov Dynasty, Russia had become more and more home to Mennonites. Based on the protection of their privileges, they were able to freely practice their faith. Even more importantly for the majority was their freedom; indeed Mennonite induced opportunity to make economic and cultural progress.

At the turn of the nineteenth to the twentieth century, Mennonites already sent their young men to Hamburg or to Switzerland to attend biblical seminars. If, however, they opted for agricultural studies or medicine, or mechanical engineering, Russian universities were recommended as well.

And so, at the beginning of the twentieth century, we find Mennonite students attending universities in Russia, Germany and in Switzerland. These young intellects displayed increasing interest, and indeed involvement in matters of nationalism in Europe; they also started pondering matters regarding their own identity. Who are we? Are we Dutch, Friesians, Swiss, Austrians, Germans or Russians?

In order to answer such questions, a commission of investigation was appointed. However, no single or satisfactory answer was readily available. Approximately half of the Mennonite names in Russia were Dutch. Others had north or south German, Swiss or Austrian roots. While still in Russia, Mennonites became ever more conscious of their status as a people, with ready and handy terms of definition failing to satisfy those of independent thinking or the educated among them.

The fact that Russia increasingly turned away from Germany politically, favoring France instead and that in the highest circles of government in Petersburg belief was prevalent that a confrontation between Austria-Germany versus Russia-France Balkan involvement was not only inevitable, and the likelihood of armed conflict a given, was a fact which almost totally escaped Mennonites. Many now realized that their status of identity as a people called for resolution.

The First World War with all its consequences called for an urgent resolution of this problem. The ever increasing relationships of Mennonites to Germany, and the deliberate cultivation of things German, particularly the German language, led to the Russian nationalists regarding them ever more as enemies of the state. Much more seriously, though, was the fact that the new power group within Communism regarded them as Kulaks (land owners), who were to be totally exterminated.

Since Mennonites had always relied on the protection of autocratic rulers, they eagerly looked for protective officials to safeguard their interests after the Communist Revolution. Since the Communist leaders in the Kremlin were explicitly a threat to the Mennonite people, the latter scouted about for more favored status among the ruling countries of Europe. Now, suddenly and certainly conveniently,

Mennonites became Hollanders once more. While doing so, they were not aware that claiming to be Netherlanders would have been more accurate, if at all, since Hollanders refers only to the people of that province within the Netherlands, even if this mistake in terminology is common and wide-spread. Official letters in matters of resolution of citizenship were now addressed to the Queen of the Netherlands; Her Majesty ignored the pleas and pleads of those, who, as usual, appealed to high-ups to resolve their own indecision or, indeed, ambiguity.

After the serious famine of 1920-21, which came about due to very short-sighted measures of the early and inexperienced Soviet government, the Communist leadership in 1922, re-directed its economic policies (NEP). In order to improve the economy, farmers were again temporarily allowed to operate independently. Without state controls, the food crisis was very quickly remedied.

Since the Mennonites had lost their patron, the Czar, and therewith also their highly touted privileges, and since emigrating was but a dim possibility, they were forced to come to terms with the new power order in the Kremlin. If the Mennonites had not been so uncompromising in matters of materialism and gains thereof, there might have been negotiating room and concessions granted. However, such was contrary to their faith, their view of the world and their inherent ideology.

Father later stated that many of the Mennonite farmers had been prepared to join the communes and cultivate the land collectively. Volunteer

Mennonite productive cooperatives during those years, few as they were, produced one record crop after another. However, such was not the intent or aim of materialistic Communism. It intended to produce a new atheistic man according to its own image and ideology. To that end, old values and institutions had to be radically eradicated, and with it the representatives of that world view were also permanently sidelined or forever muted.

By 1928 the temporary easing of the Communist economic policies were history. Stalin mobilized every measure to re-make Russia into an industrialized Communist state. This initial Five-Year-Plan was the main reason why Mennonites and other German settlers desperately sought to go to Moscow and, from there, depart the land. Among them were the future Fernheimer, to which belonged Jacob and Elisabeth Isaak and their three sons.

During the first days and weeks many of the Auhagen settlers on their estate shared a fate similar to the Children of Israel after their remarkable salvation from the Egyptian enslavement in their time. They walked through the Red Sea, while the Mennonites walked through the Red Gate. And, finally, they were free.

But what does freedom really mean in the middle of a desert without food or water, or, for that matter, the impenetrable wilderness of the Chaco Bush? Both are unconditionally delivered unto God's redemptive plan. Security and future are a given only through trust in God and in faith that God will keep His promise. In addition to their faith in God's redemptive plan, the Fernheimer had the MCC pledge that it would not forsake the settlers.

Jacob and Elisabeth Isaak (father and mother) stood before the entrance to their tent. Their thinking is alike: Finally and at last, we are free to live our faith without fear, and to commence constructing a community of the Children of God.

But how? The unlimited freedom in the bush of the Chaco does not translate to bread on the table. It does not fashion shelter from the wild thunder storms in summer. And while it soothes the soul, heart and mind, it provides no shelter from the icy south winds in winter. Have we gained our freedom only to die of famine and thirst in the wilderness, now was a burning question and an urgent issue.

The transition from the beautiful farmyard of Karlovka (Memrik) with a pleasant climate, to the tropical heat and dry earth of the Gran Chaco was radical indeed. Toward the end of November 1929, they arrived in Germany. After more than a seven month subsequent stay in Germany, they boarded a ship on July 12, and arrived in Asuncion on August 15, 1930. Upon arrival, an official reception in the capital city was held, after which they traveled on to Puerto Casado, where they arrived on August 17.

The initial trip with a very slow freight train through the Chaco was interesting enough. Palm patches, interspersed with salt lagoons and occasional islands of bush were new, soon commonplace.

Finally they arrived on August 15 at Kilometer 145 Station, where Mennos already awaited them with

Mother, father and Jacob and Gerhard in front of their house in Karlovka.

Franz Wiebe, who transported our parents from the train station to their Auhagen Settlement Camp.

ox carts to transport them to Settlement Camp Number 9. No fewer than a dozen wagons then took the 22 families to the Auhagen Camp, where they were meant to settle. This trip by ox caravan was slow in the extreme but highly interesting and educational.

A hundred questions arose as to the variety of trees and bushes and other plants of the Chaco bush. Late evenings at the camp fire close to the feeding stations, the questions asked were unending. During the trip, further questions were asked and bandied about. Father wanted to know what all could be planted and raised in the Chaco. The Menno-Man, whom the children called "Mr. Wiebe" or simply Franz Wiebe, or more simply yet, Franz, to the adults, answered all questions simply but persuasively.

Franz Wiebe, our guide had the driest sense of humor, and so his remarks and observations were welcomed with laughter, resounding deeply into the Chaco bushes. "No, wheat cannot be grown in the Chaco; too hot in summer and too dry in winter."

Then he spoke about cotton, kefir, beans, and peanuts, about manioca, and sweet potatoes and all manner of cultures which we knew only through word of mouth. Also fruits grow in the Chaco, the names of which have a strange ring to them, interspersed as they are, with English terminology. And so he constantly has to explain what the intent and purpose of the various cultures are and what purpose there is in their growth. When narrator Franz mentions watermelons, the children's eyes light up, for these they know. Yes, we know them from home. And they were that big, so big, as, say a child's head. Mr. Wiebe then smiles knowingly while stating that watermelons in the Chaco weigh up to 45 pounds, five times the size of their Russian counterparts. That claim rendered the little boys speechless. Such being the case, life in the Chaco is probably manageable after all. After a long day's journey, we finally arrive at the Auhagen Settler Camp.

After the few personal effects have been unloaded in the high bitter grass, Mr. Wiebe takes leave of us in Low German, "Look, this will be your new home." ("Hiea send Jie nu Tus!"), he said. After the caravan of wagons has disappeared in the narrow lane of the bush, tears of consternation flow and exclamations fill the air, "What? We are meant to live in this barren wilderness?"

Indeed, such was the inescapable fact. There was no way back for the Auhagen settlers. Until such time as the settlers would fully accept Mr. Wiebe's comment, "See, this will be your new home" much time would pass.

The thickly matted Chaco bush appeared to them like a desert full of thorns, without roads, without water. Nowhere was the flow of a gentle brook to be heard, or the roar of a river. Even the natural water puddles dry up within weeks or months under the merciless heat of the Chaco sun, the cold, dry south winds, or the glaring hot northern storms.

They already had had their fill of this monotonous misery during the train ride and then more of the same, but slower still, on the ramshackle ox carts.

In order to survive in this wilderness, water is an urgent necessity. Wells have to be dug at a depth of eight to ten meters. At that depth, good water is to be found, even if in sparse quantity. However, only one or two out of ten wells dug with great cooperative effort, by spade and shovel, and constant danger to life and limb, produce acceptable and potable water.

The Auhagen Tent Village was established in the proximity of such a well. However, after a short while, the good water of this well ran dry and the well produced only salt water. New wells had to be dug, with most producing water so salty, that even the cattle failed to drink it.

Finally, good water is found and much of it. However, this well is located on a palm grove, some one and one half kilometers from the tent village. A wider path is cleared in the bush by the men with axes and spades. The water is now transported by

A path through the bush. Passable only by pedestrians and riders.

yokes placed on the shoulders of men and women alike and manually carried, since horse drawn wagons were not yet available.

Let us permit our father to have the word as he did on September 29, 1971 upon the occasion of the Auhagen anniversary.

It was towards the end of 1929 when a feverish activity broke out among the Russian Mennonites. The measures taken by the government, to be carried out in a Five Year Plan were such that many families saw themselves forced to leave their Russian home on account of their faith and to search for other, more hospitable lands. There were thousands, who in September, October and November of that year fled their houses and villages and headed for Moscow. Among these were the 22 families, who later were to found the village of Auhagen, and who managed, with God's help, to travel to Germany.

However, we were not permitted to stay in Germany. We had to move on. We, as refugees, found temporary shelter in the refugee camps of Hammerstein, Prenzlau and Mőlln and were provided with food and the necessities of life. After thorough medical check-ups, a small group of healthy families was allowed to migrate to Canada. These departed at the beginning of 1930.

The large majority of these refugees, however, were not allowed to depart for Canada. Other countries were now sought out for them to settle in. The German government insisted that we depart the country. Professor B. Unruh, and the MCC worked feverishly on the lookout for alternative countries to settle in, and succeeded in receiving permission for 1000 to 1500 persons to leave for Brazil to establish new homes and at that, in short order.

But yet again, only the refugees of good health were allowed to depart. We were shown film excerpts of the areas of potential settlement in the Santa Catarina Mountains of Brazil, and the impenetrable jungles surrounding them; also we were informed of the difficulties of settling in this region. The potential hardships of settling in this area were such that I decided against migrating to Brazil with my family.

In the interim, Paraguay had opened its doors to all Mennonites, with every privilege extended for young and old, healthy or sick. The region for potential settlement, however, was the uncultivated, devoid of humanity, wild Gran Chaco which, depicted on a map, was nothing but a huge wilderness. When I saw that veritable vacuum and contemplated how we would settle there, and eke out a living and develop an existence in the wilderness of the Chaco bush, and to break that forbidding land, a nameless fear overcame me. I hesitated in my decision to head for Paraguay, particularly since I and my family had in the interim received permission of residency in Germany for an extended period.

The MCC, and also various European relief organizations, worked hard and with dedication on our behalf. They collected money and equipment to enable the emigrants to Paraguay to start afresh with greater promise and to ensure the settlers a promising start.

This equipment consisted of a tent tarpaulin measuring 6 × 6 meters; a team of oxen for every two farms, a wagon for every four farms, as well as one plough, a harrow, a cultivator, and two large hoes, a small garden hoe, a scythe, a bush scythe for every two farms, a machete, an axe, a spade, a pickaxe for every two farms, a lantern and, upon arrival in Paraguay, one zinc barrel per farm.

In addition, we were promised kitchen equipment and furnishings. These consisted of a hot plate, two cast iron casseroles, a broiler pan, three bowls, a plate each, a cup, a knife, a fork and a spoon per person, three enameled casseroles, a ladle, a meat grinder for every four people, a sewing machine and a cauldron for every six farms.

This was indeed a huge and practical aid and we had every reason to be thankful. In addition, the MCC provided full board for one year as well as assistance and financial aid for the start-up period. The MCC promised to stand guard for brotherly assistance for the period of initial settlement. True to their word, the MCC invariably honored its every promise.

After the matter of equipment had been resolved, Prof. H.S. Bender, on behalf of the MCC, and Prof. B. Unruh, appeared before the refugees and commenced advertising recruitment of Paraguay to the settlers. It was not long before the first lot was fully prepared and sent on its way. These consisted of settlers for the villages 1, 2 and half of 3. After a few weeks, the second group was also full up: the villages half of 3, 4 and 5. And again after a few weeks the third group was ready: the villages 6, 7 and 8 ready for take-off. The fourth and final group consisted of villages 9, 10 and 11.

Bronze plates with the names of the Auhagen settlers inscribed.

The allotments of settlers for the respective villages was already arranged in Germany by drawing lots. The village mayors were already chosen in Germany as well. The election for village #9, the later Auhagen chose Julius Tőws for its mayor. The name Auhagen was chosen to honor Prof. Auhagen, who in Moscow dedicated himself selflessly for the refugees. 22 families consisting of 107 persons were settled on 22 farms in Auhagen.

When the Mennos, consisting of 22 families were debarked, and made their way to their new home, many questions arose, and more tears were shed, "Are we to remain here? Are we really meant to settle and live here?" The temporary tent village

The heads of Auhagen families, comprising the village community, organized in Germany. The second from the right in the second row is our father.

called Chuta was laid out close to the well. Since the strange and somewhat hostile wilderness in which "wild Indians" supposedly roamed appeared frightening, the tents were pitched in close proximity to each other. Nothing of danger transpired. The Indians failed to appear and we even dared to enter the bush.

The first and hard discovery we made was the well: it had but little water. It was totally insufficient. We possessed neither wagon teams nor barrels, and so we had to fetch the water from a well one and one half kilometer distance.

The first common initiative by the village community was the digging of more wells. More than a dozen wells dug on the village camp were unsuccessful in that they produced only salty water. Finally, at two kilometers distance a well was dug which produced much good water.

Then the land had to be surveyed and the village plan had to be laid out. The small camp was meant to accommodate 22 farmsteads, with each stead measuring 65 meters in width. The *length of each farmstead varied greatly. These measured 460 meters, but only 4 farmsteads actually had the allotted space.*

Towards the end of September and the beginning of October, we took occupancy of our allotment in the village, with each family assuming its farmstead, as determined by drawing of lots. A picturesque tent village now propped up. The wood for the frame of the tents was hewn in the bush and carried on human shoulders to the building sites. After the construction of the tents, the furnishings were undertaken. Oh my, this was an art unto itself! These rail beds, measured 70 to 80 cm in width and 1.5 to 2.0 meters in length. A straw bag was placed on these rails, and shortly we slept in heavenly peace. Our benches were made out of palosanto timber, and we carved the chairs out of bottle tree wood.

During October and November and December we received our allotted beast of burden oxen; also every family received a cow, but no milk. This was one year in coming. Once we received the oxen, we had to domesticate them and get them fit for harness. The young boys of the village enjoyed this breaking in a great deal; all this was new and represented a challenge, albeit roughshod and not without danger. Thank God, all this transpired without any serious accidents. Soon the ox teams were ready to travel to the train station to fetch the supplies of life.

We received our groceries once monthly including flour, rice, oil or fat, sugar, beans and meat. The portions were small. The allotments for families consisting of adults only, were meager. The Paraguayan beans were not tasty, but they proved nutritional and gradually we came to like them.

When the rain season came in October, November and December we started seeding. We had cleared a patch of five by seven meters, and dug it up with spade and hoe. We planted our first peanuts on this patch. Then we plowed one acre with

The tent village where the entire family set out to work the fields.

our oxen, and planted cotton, beans and kefir; the autumn harvest was good.

Families with grown-up children were the first in erecting homes. First, a frame of timber was constructed and covered with reeds or bitter grass. The walls were then fashioned out of bundles of bitter grass, immersed in clay. These bundles were suspended over zinc wire or round wood and then knitted together, and, in this way, an air tight wall was fashioned. At times, the walls were made with air dried bricks. Still others mixed bitter grass with clay and kneaded them in forms constructed out of wood, placed layer upon layer. Palo Blanco was split and then flattened on three sides with an axe and a plane. This manner of wood manufacture enabled the construction of windows and door frames. The first families managed to move into their new homes by Christmas of 1930, while we only managed to complete our house in 1931.

Shortly, every farmer was required to construct a fence parallel to the village street. Work done communally as required by vil-

An ox team plowing.

A transport of goods. Here, two ox teams are teamed up in tandem to drag a wagon out of the mud.

The inside of a tent equipped with round wood and reeds.

lage order, expedited an enclosure surrounding the entire village camp. The local Indians helped us in chopping fence posts and in clearing the camp to that end.

At the end of November 1930 Grandpa Julius Martens died. The coffin was shaped out of a bottle tree with the corpse being placed in it. He was buried at the edge of the bush on a plot designated to be the cemetery. His wife died a few months later and was buried next to him.

At the beginning of 1932, war between Paraguay and Bolivia broke out. In short order, military units arrived in our villages. Some of them were stationed west of our village. Since the discipline in the Paraguayan military ranks was strict, no one in our village was molested by the soldiers. The military shot the Indians arbitrarily since they were held to be spies.

We were able to get on with operating our farms, constructing our houses and tilling the soil. Then, one day the dreaded news spread to the effect that all settlers were to be evacuated. We were gravely concerned. How was this to be realized? We had only one wagon for four families. Would we yet again lose what we had so meticulously constructed?

Prayer meetings were conducted in our villages, appealing to God to spare us this tragedy. The Lord responded. The next morning we received news that the evacuation had been suspended. We were happy, and indeed thankful.

Since three acres of land per family was insufficient, the surrounding camps were surveyed and rendered fertile. This increased our holdings to five acres per family; the crops were good.

Transporting necessary goods and necessities to and from the train station presented an immense problem. During the dry season, it took a week to make the trip by ox-team; during the rainy season the roads turned to seas of mud and such trips lasted for weeks on end.

Men operating a cross saw.

There were many children in our various village settlements and as many teenagers. School instruction commenced in the shade of trees, within weeks after they arrived.

In 1934, the first school was built, the largest in the settlement. In short order, young men and women fell in love and married. Further, from the very beginning, prayer meetings were conducted on Saturday nights. Church services were initially conducted in the shade of trees, then in private homes and later in the large school. There were good singers to be found among the young people. At their request, I organized a choir with two weekly choir practices and we sang at the Sunday church service.

We had already been informed in Germany that it was impossible to work with horses in the Chaco; this proved to be untrue. Soon after our arrival the first horses and mules were purchased for our farms. The amount of plow-able land then promptly increased to nine acres per farm.

In 1934 we experienced our first locust infestation. Since the crop had already been harvested by Pentecost, the damages were

Construction of our first huts.

A house typical of the beginning of settlement. Children on an ox-cart, with chickens and pigs roaming about. The family engaged in eating a giant sized watermelon.

Photo of Palo Blanco: Quebracho (axe breaker) tree on a typical animal pasture.

The military during the Chaco War; a military unit was stationed in Auhagen; the commander paid our school a visit. Back left, Teacher Gerhard Rempel, with Gerhard Isaak standing front right.

Gerhard mounted on a horse with Cornelius, Heinrich and Jacob in front of our first adobe house in Auhagen, 1934.

minimal. However, it was much worse when the locusts returned in November to lay their eggs in our every vegetation. When the young hatched three weeks later, the battle against this infestation was almost hopeless. Wide and deep ditches were excavated which the young locusts found insurmountable.

Then the locusts were driven into the ditches and covered with soil. These nasty jumpers formed huge swarms which covered hundreds of square meters. The swarms moved, or, actually rolled on in whatever arbitrary direction and destroyed everything in their path. Alarms were posted and every hand, big and small, was engaged in fighting them off. Then the caterpillars arrived and, worse still, the ants. Step by step, we learned to fight them off or at least control them so that the damages were kept to a minimum.

In 1937 a group of settlers departed the Chaco to re-settle in East Paraguay in the Colony of Friesland; none of the families from Auhagen joined this group.

In 1937 father and mother decided to purchase two farms in the neighboring village #14, Blumenort, thereby managing to acquire more land, a necessity for a growing family.

Father plowing and mother casting seed on the loose soil.

Peanut transport on wagons.

Evening has come. Father and mother again sit in front of the tent. They have fashioned simple but comfortable chairs from bottle tree wood. The great heat of the day has abated, but it is still sultry. There is sheet lightning on the southwesterly horizon. Will the much anticipated rain finally come? Father has checked the tent guide lines because the rain from southerly directions is generally accompanied by storms.

The small peanut field measuring 7 × 10 meters looks good. Cotton, beans and kefir have come up and are in need of a good rain.

They are discussing the affairs of the day. That morning our parents had started making clay bricks. After arduous labor, they had managed to fashion several hundred bricks and pile them up for the sun to dry. Tin panels were borrowed to cover the bricks in case of rain. Their sons already managed to assist in the labors of the day and even enjoyed doing so. They were allowed to play in and with the clay which required kneading, then mixing for the manufacture of adobe bricks.

Every so often, their thoughts hark back to Russia. How may their parents and siblings fare? From the Hildebrandt and Isaak clan, only Jacob and Elisabeth were fortunate enough to escape. Letters exchanged took much time and frequently remained unanswered. Russia still remained their home. It is there where they spent their childhood, their youth and the first years of marriage.

The Gerhard Isaak farmyard in Lindenau, Russia where father was born. From left to right: Heinrich, Gerhard, Mary, Heinrich's wife with their children, Lena, Cornelius, father's parents, the Gerhard Isaaks.

Again, we let our father have the word as to how, on September 5, 1949, he reflected on their Silver Wedding Anniversary in Karlsruhe.

In 1 Samuel 7:12 we read, "Then Samuel took a stone and set it up between Mitzpeh and Shen. He named it Ebenezer, saying, Thus far the Lord has helped us." Ebenezer is what we say today, my dear wife and I. Truly, up to here and now, the Lord has helped us. The Lord has done great things unto us and we rejoice therein.

Today we want to tell about the honor of God and our lives. It was on October 8, 1900, when I first saw the light of day in our beautiful village of Lindenau. My parents were Gerhard and Maria Isaak, nee Mantler. We had a full-sized farm of some 160 acres and prior to the Revolution, we farmed an equal amount of rented land.

I was the eighth child of my parents. After me, another three children were born. There were eleven children in our family. Three of the siblings, Anna, Tina and Cornelius died in their infancy. The other eight children survived into adulthood. Chronologically this was the series of siblings: Gerhard, Helen, Peter, Heinrich, Hans, Maria and I, and, after me, another Cornelius followed.

In my memory, my childhood was bright and sunny. I grew up under the loving care of my parents and siblings. In time, I attended the two classroom school in Lindenau which was located in our neighborhood. I was fortunate to complete this school without any change of teachers till my thirteenth year.

Upon the wish of my parents and siblings, I passed the entrance examination to the Orloff High School in May 1914. The school year was to begin in the autumn of that year. However, man proposes while God disposes. The affairs of men and life transpired differently from expectations.

In August, like a thunderbolt from clear skies, the dreaded news arrived: War had broken out! As of this moment, the peaceful life and existence of Mennonite villages and colonies were forever gone. Then followed the second piece of terrible news: mobilization of active military, then, in short order, reserves as well. This meant that all men between 20 and 40 had to serve in the Russian army. Initially Mennonite men were spared service due to previous privileges extended.

However, shortly thereafter, these were also enlisted to serve as orderlies of the sick and wounded. This order immediately affected my three older brothers, and they had to heed the call of the government, with my oldest brother having to go to the high north to work under arduous conditions in a lumber camp.

Suddenly my father was left alone to look after a large farm. He left it to me to decide as to whether I would attend high school in Orloff, or remain at home. Like most boys of my age, who make stupid decisions, so did I. I decided to stay at home, ostensibly to help my father. In truth it was freedom "out there" that attracted me.

The discipline of school appeared too demanding to me. Furthermore, schooling demanded hard work. By staying at home, I could avoid all such demands. After a year of loitering about, I was ready for school, but it was too late. I had to wait till the war was over. Then, in 1917, a school of advanced education was opened in our village. This was my opportunity to return to school, which I completed after two years.

In 1919 I enrolled in the Politechnicum Kopodorkux in Berdyansk. This school had been transferred from Dnepropetrovsk to Berdyansk under the Denikin Reign. I was able to study here for a year in peace and quiet and I experienced a very happy time of my life. Berdyansk is situated on the Sea of Azov, with a beautiful spa and with vineyards surrounding it; it will remain a happy memory. However, no eternal bond can be smithied with fate's decree, and misfortune hovers eternally (Schiller).

For a while now, unsettling news circulated in the city. We heard about peasant revolts in the principalities of Dnepropetrovsk and Taurien, with these rumors persisting. These rumors, very shortly, were confirmed as fact.

It was not long before revolts spread to our city. The small garrison of our city attempted to fend off the Machnovtse with cannons and machine guns. However, the marauding bands chose an alternate route. They moved along the seashore, then crossing into the city via the suburbs, where many mutinously inclined citizens were waiting to join in the revolts.

When these rebels also shortly joined the Machnovtse, they entered the cities before the military could defend them. Street battles raged, but they lasted only a few hours. Soon the division of the White Army departed and Berdyansk was left to the terror of the roving bands.

After a few weeks, word spread that classes in the schools would recommence. We resumed our studies, but concentrated studies were out of the question; things were simply too revolutionary. News of the terror that the bands executed in our villages and colonies was most alarming.

One day three of us Mennonite students gathered to discuss the matter. We agreed that one of us ought to go home to gather reliable facts. I was chosen to go, and I decided to go home at the very first opportunity. I heard that a train was due to depart shortly for Feodorowka. This information was confirmed in the train station. I prayed for God's protection and presence en route.

The next evening I boarded the train. In the compartment, there were some ten to fifteen people who made a most unfavorable impression on me. The train finally departed after a few hours only to be derailed after a few minutes. It started off again but only after hours of waiting. When daylight broke and I awoke, I noticed that I was in the midst of a gang of drunken Machnovtse; I was very afraid. Once again I found consolation and assurance in prayer to God, and He responded to my supplication.

Since our locomotive was heated by wood and it was slow at the best of times, it took till the evening of the day until we arrived at the juncture of Werni-Tokmak, where we stayed overnight. I had the opportunity to see the leader of the revolutionary army Batjko Machnov. He was drunk, and just returned from Great Tokmak where he had shot the great Jewish merchant Tekker. With a revolver in hand, he swayed drunkenly, assisted by two of his fellows as he passed me by. While stumbling along he uttered the terrible words, "Cut them all, the dead and also the living."

The protective hand of God kept this bloodhound in the

station for only a few minutes before he departed. One of the leaders of the revolts confided in me that things did not bode well for their cause and that they would not prevail.

I did not sleep well that night. Again and again I prayed that God would take me home safe and sound. God answered my prayer. The next morning, the train resumed its journey, and I arrived home safely before evening. I managed to arrive home in time to bid my brother Hans farewell. He was assigned to take a number of horses, which the revolutionaries had picked, to Amelik. En route, Hans was murdered. We managed to retrieve his corpse only after two months and properly bury him.

I was at home now and I would gladly have returned the next day but that was out of the question. My studies had come to an abrupt end.

A horrible time had come for the Mennonite colonies. A horde of evil marauders terrorized the inhabitants of the villages; they robbed, burned, murdered and raped.

As if paralyzed by death or frozen by terror, the good people of our villages were incapable of stopping the bloodshed. In the coming four to five weeks, many of our women and girls were raped, and hundreds of our men murdered. My brother Hans was one of the victims.

(Explanation: Father makes no mention of the highly controversial Mennonite Self-Defense. So much is certain today: some 2,000 Mennonite young men organized and armed themselves, and under the command of German officers, temporarily protected Mennonite villages).

Finally, this reign of terror came to an end after a few months. The war-front between the Whites (the army of the Czar) and the Reds (Communist) came ever closer, and just before Christmas, our villages were under Red rule.

We now had a government again, and a certain sense of order and security prevailed, with the Reds having put a decisive end to the marauding bands. In exchange, we had to provide living quarters for the military, as well as providing provisions.

We finally had a semblance of peace, but the Whites had not been totally beaten. Once more General Wrangel mounted an attack from the Crimea, but the Reds beat him back, and before the end of the year, they were in command of the entire Russian empire. It did not take long before we became acquainted with the rule of the Soviet regime.

For a time we fared rather well; we were no longer unduly mistreated. The churches were again allowed to practice their faith. When in spring catechism classes commenced, I also became a member of the baptismal class. Baptism was due on Pentecost Day. However, I still had not committed myself to Jesus Christ; I was not a committed Christian. I found my sins and guilt bothersome. And then, one night I managed to attain the forgiveness of my sins through the immense grace of God based on the cross of Jesus Christ and I received healing. "All you have to do is believe," a voice in me announced and faith entered. I knew that my sins were forgiven. In the faith in Jesus Christ, the son of God and my personal savior, I was baptized by Bishop Bernhard Epp on Pentecost Day of 1920, and I became a member of the Lichtenauer Congregation.

Since then I have been a follower of Jesus Christ. Unfortunately I did not always remain steadfast in my faith, I must admit. To follow the Word, "Let us cast aside all sins", brought hard struggles with it, but I attained victory in time. I was able to experience the truth of the Word. "If the Son sets you free, you will be free indeed" (John 8:36). Thank God! This did not transpire overnight; it was a long, hard struggle.

In 1921, because of great drought and chaotic economic policies of the new Communist government, a total crop failure visited all of South Russia. There were no grain reserves whatsoever. A great famine was inevitable.

All we had for our large family were some 1800 pounds of wheat and a few pounds of other grains. This prompted me to set out by horse and wagon for the Cuban area together with my brother's brother in law, Hans Wiens. From there we proceeded on to the Mennonite settlements in the Terek area. The unannounced aim of our trip, however, was America. After 17 days travel we arrived at Weliko Knjaschesk in the Cuban.

There we found twelve large Mennonite villages. These farmers were wealthy and knew little about the revolution, and had suffered little. We remained here for the next four to five weeks. Then we joined a group of back settlers on their way to the Terek Settlement. These had fallen prey to the Obrek raiders.

We formed a group of five travelers, but now five more joined us on our wagon, so that we were a party of ten on one wagon.

In December we arrived at the Terek Settlement, where I immediately was engaged as a tutor. I was well looked after and enjoyed both good food and fine lodgings. Later, when things became poor at my host's place as well, I became a tutor to a wealthy Tartar family. I worked there in this capacity until Easter.

After Easter we sold our wagon and the team of horses and made our way to Batum, a port on the Black Sea close to the Turkish border. It was here that a group of Mennonite families had gathered over time; this group comprised of some 250 persons. They had come from the Molotsch area, from the Old Colony, and from Crimea and all had fled the famine and were now looking for ways to migrate to America. Unfortunately, plans to depart were postponed for months on end. When typhoid broke out, some 40 of this group died. At times so many were sick, that there were not enough men available to bury the dead. Then there was no recourse but for the women to dig the graves.

Malaria also broke out among us. I also fell ill with typhoid. During the third attack I got spotty typhoid and was admitted to hospital where I lay unconscious for 14 days. My time of death had not yet come. I recovered and soon had yet another job in the city. We continued to wait for a chance to sail for America; things turned out much differently. I contracted such a severe case of malaria that my doctors advised me to leave Batum or risk death.

It was now already December 1922, and Hans Wiens and I decided to leave for home. We joined a group of Mennonite refugees who intended to head for home in a collective transport. However, Hans and I did not go home but, instead, de-boarded the train in Ebental in the Memrik Colony and spent Christmas at my Uncle Johann Isaak's home.

From there I went on to Ossokino to visit my brother Peter Isaak, and my sister Maria, who lived there since her wedding with her husband. Her husband, my brother in law, was Heinrich Mantler. My brother had long since invited me to pay him a visit but I had simply not wanted to do so. Now the Lord had changed my attitude and direction.

It was here that I became acquainted with a young girl, who greatly appealed to me at first glance and to whom I felt attracted to. In the course of time we became closer. When I asked her one day if she would be my wife, she consented. Her name was Elisabeth Hildebrandt, my present very dear wife. In the course of 25 years she has been a loyal mate, a good partner indeed, in good days as well as in bad, she has always been a faithful woman.

One day, after she had consented to marry me, we visited her parents. When we informed them of our love, and asked for their blessings, they gladly gave them to us. We celebrated our engagement in a small circle. Since the harvest of the season was imminent, our wedding was postponed by two months.

Mother's photo on her refugee identity certificate in a German camp.

Our engagement, which lasted two months, was a wonderfully good time. Harvest time had arrived. We could not be together all that often due to pressures of work, but it was a glorious and happy time. Even now, we reflect often and happily on that joyous time.

Finally, the day arrived on which we united for the rest of our lives. That day was August 24, or September 5, 1924 depending on the calendar (Russia had a different calendar, adjusting it to the West after the Revolution), and a truly beautiful late summer day it was. Many visitors arrived from far and near to share our happiness. Among them was our dear bishop Jacob Pätkau from Memrik, who officiated at the formal part of our wedding vows. He had chosen Psalm 84:12-13 as the wedding text which was certainly appropriate and which constantly came to mind over the years as timely. It reads: "God our Lord is a sun and shield. The Lord gives grace and glory. O Lord of hosts, blessed is the man who trusts in Him!"

My dear Elisabeth had also found the Lord and was shortly thereafter accepted by baptism into the Memrik Mennonite Church. And thus we shared a common ground of faith and were able to bend our knees to the same Lord and Savior to this day. Through Jesus Christ, God our Father in Heaven is the sun of our life. His grace, power and love form the shield which has protected us in the hour of great danger to body and soul. The Lord has been with us in rich measure. And with grace we also received honor, although we never sought it out; we can state that with an honest heart.

We never suffered for lack of goodness, and must freely confirm this. It is indeed true: "It is well for man to depend on the Lord." "Turn your ways unto the Lord" was a call I received in a very serious and decisive hour in my life; "...and hope for Him. He will see you through." I have done this, and so has my wife. And we experienced His response. The Lord honors His promises and He keeps His Word.

We entered our marriage on the true foundation of the Life of Jesus Christ and His Word. Our bishop Jacob Pätkau (who became a victim of the Soviets in the Thirties) blessed us with these very words.

We became one out of two and we happily enjoyed the sun of our happiness. Unfortunately, the times were such that we could not afford to fashion our own hearth. We stayed with our parents in law and remained with them for the first five years of our life, sharing space under the same roof. My wife was the only daughter of the family. Her only brother shortly followed our example and also married. And so we two young couples lived together with the parents and fared quite well.

But not for long. The political conditions were such that we were forced to sell our beautiful and prosperous estate and to find an alternate site to dwell and make a living. We found it in the Memrik Colony in the village of Karlovka. This well situated village with a creek, Wolschja, with good neighbors and a huge garden was available for purchase.

In retrospect, this was a foolish decision. We should have migrated to Canada at that time. And yet, Russia was beautiful and good and had become our earthly home. Everything would work out in time. The revolution and the famine were over. We thought in those terms and we believed it and acted accordingly. The new economic policies led to a great boom in short order. Until 1917, we believed in a good future in Russia and felt sorry for those who had left the country. It was particularly the old, experienced farmers who chose not to clearly assess the political realities of the day.

However, we of the younger generation, who read the printed media and followed the Communist party line, were not nearly *as optimistic about the future in this country. We knew that our faith and our Christian life were in jeopardy; there were dark clouds hovering on a distant horizon and we knew it. Based on such deliberations, we cast about seriously in 1926 and 1927, looking for ways to depart the country and immigrate. However, all doors to that end were shut.*

At this time the local church asked me to start work on a small scale with the young people. We staged programs with songs and poetry recitals and we worked for the Lord in humble beginnings. When our minister in 1926 departed for Canada, I was chosen to become an evangelist, or, more accurately an itinerant minster. I felt too incompetent for this position and refused to assume it. While I served my church as best I could, I was mindful of my limitations. I lacked an unconditional dedication to the work, unfortunately.

In the meanwhile, it was obvious how things were going and it was our wish and supplication to God to hear our prayers since our needs became ever more pressing. We prayed that He find a way for us and our children to immigrate. Things became so urgent and pressing, that one day I made a vow to God: If you will lead me and my family out of this land, I will serve you anywhere, anyhow, wherever you may need me. The Lord answered this prayer and in the beginning of 1929 He led us across the Soviet borders and to freedom abroad.

Together with many others, who likewise became benefactors of His grace, we left for Germany via Eidkuhnen. After an eight month stay in Germany, the Lord directed us into the Chaco of Paraguay.

Here in the Chaco Wilderness, after extremely difficult beginnings, I soon had a chance to honor my previous vow to God made in Russia! The first call for me to become a minister of the Word came in Germany. The second call to serve Him now

Open air worship service.

came in Paraguay. I have to confess that I did not immediately respond. I was conscious of my weaknesses. Was I worthy of taking His Word into my hands and into my mouth? We prayed a lot on this matter.

Then one day it became clear to me: It is the Lord who is calling you. When He then reminded me of my vow, I agreed to the call. My weaknesses were many and powerful and my hesitation no less when I commenced my work. And yet, I must admit that the Lord blessed my modest efforts from the outset as I performed my duty. I did the best I could in the knowledge that He would honor whatever I did, be it ever so small and modest, if done in the name of Jesus, our Lord and Savior of this world, and our faith and confidence in Him would be blessed. My dear wife, and later my children never were an impediment in my work; they invariably pushed and supported my every endeavor, even if at times I would have preferred to remain at home.

The Word of our Lord, "He who has, much will be given, so that he will have even more," found fulfillment with us in many *ways. The promise of the marital text, "The Lord provides grace and honor. He will spare nothing good to the pious," went fulfilled in our life. "Lord God, be well unto mankind, which depends on you. Amen!"*

CHAPTER II
Family and Church Life Assume Contours

OUR FATHER WAS ALREADY elected minister in Russia. However, he declined the call since he felt too weak for the office. When the calamity of the very existence became all too consuming in Russia, he made a vow to God, "If you will deliver me and my family from Russia into a free land, I will serve you, wherever you may call me!"

While in Germany, his spiritual gifts again came to be noticed. It was there when he was boarding the ship, that an inner voice announced, "Jake, if they call you to the ministry, do not decline!"

Mother was born in Ossokino in 1901 as the only daughter of Gerhard and Elizabeth (Gooszen) Hildebrandt. The Hildebrandts owned an estate, meaning they were wealthy. She grew up in a family with her brother Cornelius; they had a rich supply of everything required to live well. This does not mean that the siblings were spoiled, far from it. They were required to get up early to work just like their parents and their Russian servants. No exceptions, no privileges extended when it came to working in the house, in the stable or in the fields. They had to work just as hard and as long as all the others. And so mother learned from an early age on to treat workers as equals and how to get along with them.

Elisabeth and Cornelius Hildebrandt's family.

Her brother Cornelius grew up in like manner. On the large farmstead with its own blacksmith shop and other machine shops, he very early learned how to manage machinery and he knew their workings. Later, when he was banned to the far north of Russia, this experience stood him in good stead. His children often narrated as to how their father always found work and always made a good living and readily found food for himself and his family and how to protect his family from famine and from the elements.

Mother's childhood and youth transpired as in a dream. She was the only daughter but she was not spoiled or given preferential treatment. She was in the midst of everything on a large farm; on the yard with its many horses, cows, goats and pigs, in the hen house with the chickens, ducks and geese, in the garden with its many fruit trees and berry bushes, or on the field, where she worked from planting time till harvest and did all the hard labor alongside of all the others.

Ossokino was not spared the ravages of the First World War and the Russian Revolution. Sometimes the young, beautiful Elisabeth found herself in grave danger. Twice she managed to escape the wild roving bands at peril to life and limb.

Shortly after the Red Army brought all of Russia under its rule, an abrupt end was put to all the roving bands and peace and order was restored. Work in the house, on the yard and on the fields could again resume.

The Ossokiners were largely dependent on the Memrik Colony for their social and religious life. It was in the Twenties that a young man gained fame in this area. His name was Jacob Isaak. He organized a choir with the local Mennonite youth. Further, programs were practiced and performed. In terms of maturity and experience, he was far ahead of his contemporaries in the colony.

Even though Elisabeth claimed that she could not sing, and she rejected participation in available programs, there were many other opportunities for her to be involved in and to exchange social pleasantries. Before long, everyone knew that Jacob Isaak and Elisabeth Hildebrandt were a couple. The reading of the marital bans in church and their wedding two months later were a surprise to no one.

Mother had always had a special heart for the young and vulnerable. One day a nanny (she goat) on their farm failed to survive the birth of her kid. It was matter of course for Elisabeth to nurse the poor kid and to raise it with a bottle. For the kid, Elisabeth became the mother. It followed her every step of the way and cried woefully when its mother was not around. Like all goats, it was curious and climbed on top of everything in sight and also munched everything edible. Whether the kid was envious of father or whether it was bent on revenge for having absconded with its mother, we will never know. What we do know is that on the wedding day, when the guests assembled in the dining room, the baby goat was already there, standing on the middle of the table and eating the wedding cake.

Mother invariably remained in the background. That was always so. Mennonite women always assumed this role in matters of public affairs. This was the case in Russia and again for the first decades in Paraguay as well. There were other reasons for her reticence in matters of public concern. Mother's explanations to that end were: The Hildebrandt clan had always lived in close proximity to water. As soon as storms appear and emotions run high, water tends to run over. On occasions, she commented that there was much she would have liked to say in matters of church meetings. But, she knew that her voice would then break and tears would follow and so she preferred to simply hold her peace. In short, our mother could easily be brought to tears.

Father and mother each had their role in the family, on the yard and in public life. In such matters, tensions never arose. Father's realm was the work

The Isaak yard with a wagon and water barrel.

in church, in society, in the local and international conference and the missionary work among the Indians. Mother's realm from the very outset was in the family, the household, on the yard, and in the planning and supervision of field work, whenever father was otherwise engaged.

Whenever father returned home from a lengthy trip, his beloved Lisa received a kiss. Then she beamed like a young bride. Otherwise we children never witnessed any tender exchanges between our parents. Neither did we witness them ever quarreling, or notice any friction between them.

The experiences mother had on the Ossokino Estate stood her in very good stead when she worked with Indians in breaking the Chaco soil, when hoeing weeds, or during the cotton harvest.

Since father was mostly en route, it was obvious that mother looked after the workers. Since these were quartered on our premises for weeks on end, mother assigned them their sleeping quarters and cooked for them.

When the Indians arrived at the beginning of the harvest, they were mostly emaciated and hungry and their ribs protruded in countable formation through their wrinkled skin. Mother fed them so well that they gained weight in short order and their skin assumed healthy color and hue.

The main meal consisted of a large bone of beef with much meat and fat attached. After the bone had boiled for an hour or two in a cast iron kettle, yams, beans and other vegetables were added and then cooked for as long as it took to produce a tasty and nourishing stew. When these workers were called to lunch, their faces beamed and they stopped eating only after the stew was depleted. Some of them then plucked handfuls of wild, but very hot peppers from the edge of the bush. They enjoyed these beyond measure.

The harvested cotton was stored in a granary, some distance removed from the yard. It remained here until it could be hauled to a de-seeding station, later called a gin. On a bitterly cold winter night mother suddenly smelled smoke. When she got up to look out the window, she noticed that the cotton granary was on fire. The family was quickly awakened.

One of the boys was ordered to the village bell and to peal out the agreed-upon fire alarm. Within minutes all the adult population of the vicinity arrived at the fire scene. Both men and women of the village came running and water was fetched from the communal well. Burning cotton can hardly be contained with water. The burning upper layer has to be removed and thrown on a pile until it has been consumed by the fire.

After hours of fighting the fire, it was finally under control. When the family was finally in bed, the children heard their mother weeping. As strong, as resourceful, and as courageous as she was, there were times during which she simply did not know how she would manage.

The essentials of life were purchased from the sale of cotton; there was simply no recourse. How would our large family now be able to make do until the next crop was harvested? The next morning it was determined that a considerable amount of cotton was salvageable.

We would now have to economize even stricter, patch worn pants and skirts yet again, plant yet more vegetables and raise an additional pig, and we should somehow be able to manage. We would simply have to make do with less white flour and add more kefir flour to the dough for bread. Buns and white bread would be reduced for special occasions only. We children would have to make do with kefir porridge, with milk only and without sugar. And that is exactly what we did.

A proverb claims that whatever goods a man hauls into a barn, a woman is capable of carrying out with an apron. Mother always wore an apron. Vegetables

The Isaak farm in Blumenort in the Fifties. In the foreground a typical long-horned Creole cow is observed.

and fruit, yams and manioc, eggs and even baby chicks found their way via her apron into the kitchen of the house.

Whenever a mother hen started making clucking noises, then such clucking chirps were a sure sign that she had laid her eggs in a hidden nest in the bushes around the house. We then secretly watched her when she came to the water trough and then headed back to her nest; then the mother hen was caught and the eggs were placed in a new nest in the chicken house where they were safe from wild cats, foxes and snakes.

There the hen could brood her eggs in safety. When the chicks hatched, our mother brought them inside in her apron until all the baby chicks were hatched. Only then were the chicks entrusted to their mother hen who looked after them with much care and clucking commotion.

We children particularly enjoyed playing with the baby chicks. The youngest daughter and our sister, Irene, remembers that she repeatedly visited the hen house to determine whether the chicks were about to be hatched. When that day arrived, she ran quickly to our mother to report the news. Mother did not believe her, it was too early. But when checking the calendar, she realized that the chicks were indeed due. She took her little daughter by the hand, walking her to the hen house. And sure enough, all the eggs except one, a rotten one, were hatched and baby chicks were everywhere.

Mother deposited all twenty little chicks in her apron, took the mother hen in her one arm, and taking her daughter by the hand, they entered the warm kitchen. Now the little girl was able to fondle the velvet soft chickens with her little fingers, much to the disapproval of mother hen.

Mother was like a mother to our workers, the indigenous Indians. She managed these people of nature very well, wordlessly. It was a special honor for these men if their own wives were well nourished, or even a bit plump. Everyone can then see for themselves, and determine that they are well looked after.

Mother was a tall and sleek woman and the workers admired her for her good figure. One day one of the Indian workers paid her a compliment, saying in Mennonite Low German, words to the effect, “My senora also has fat hams”, meaning that his wife was as beautiful as our mother. Mother knew full well what he meant and she took his remark as a compliment with a broad smile. Another Mennonite man stated that he always thought of our mother as the most beautiful of women and that he had admired her when he was a young boy. In his eyes, she was the most attractive woman and mother in the entire colony.

When our parents already resided in a retirement home, it happened that the children came visiting. Since mother had already nodded off, conversations were reduced to a whisper. Father looked at mother lovingly and remarked, "Don't I have a lovely wife?" The children present confirmed that she was the most beautiful and best mother alive.

For as long as the working Indians and their families lived on our yards, mother looked after their every need. If another baby was due, mother looked after them. When babies were born, mother supplied them with a simple necessary layette. If an Indian fell ill or had an open wound or boils, mother would invariably tend to them with her home remedies. In serious cases, patients were taken to the hospital in Filadefia.

Once, while harvesting peanuts, a young much pregnant woman was present. Suddenly she disappeared, only to return with a healthy baby half an hour later. When the new mother shortly resumed her work, and mother heard about the baby, she took the young mother by the arm and tended to her and her baby in a manner previously unknown to the new mother.

Father was the head of the family. However, when he was gone on yet another mission, mother took over his role.

In addition to looking after a huge household which consisted of the parents and eleven children, she supervised all the work on the fields. Together with her boys she planned the labor and the allotting of field work every day. This might involve, depending on the time of year, plowing and planting, hoeing and exterminating vermin as well as bringing in the crops.

Mother, together with her three daughters, looked after a huge household. Whenever the weeds tended to take the upper hand, or the cotton had to be harvested before the impending rain, mother and daughters worked on the fields most efficiently.

One day of the week was mandatory laundry day. Then the old manually operated washing machine was hauled out to the yard and things started spinning. Wet but clean laundry was strung out on the long lines; clothes for a household of thirteen people demands space by many meters. Since clothes lines were fully exposed to the village street, passersby had their fun in counting all the pants, shirts, skirts and dresses. People were always impressed. Mother was happy if each child had two pairs of working clothes and one of Sunday best. No matter how many patches pants sported, the fact that they were clean is all that mattered.

For one of the boys, namely Helmut, things became a tad embarrassing when sporting a large hole in the rear of his Sunday pants, and appearing at an older brother's wedding in patched trousers.

Another of mother's responsibilities was the

milking of the cows. When every family contractually received a cow, these were mainly wild beasts. And while these produced a calf once a year or every second year, they did not become mild cows. In the course of centuries, this Creole cow had developed into a very tough breed, which prevailed in dry as well as in wet years. It survived for weeks, indeed months on end with very little feed or water. When the rains came, and there was a surplus of pasture and water, this breed quickly put on weight. It survived hordes of mosquitoes and wasps, ticks, and even plagues did not manage to bring her down.

However, when it came to milk, she produced just enough to raise her calf. These cows were also obstinate, swished their tails like a whip and kicked with every leg often and accurately and knew what horns were made for. The MCC donated this cow to the settlers, who, to this day, are thankful for receiving this Creole cow.

This practically wild cow was now left for mother to milk because milking cows was generally the responsibility of the women. This happened every morning as follows: For starters, father had to throw a rope over the cow's horns. The cow was then pulled to a post on a short leash, where the cow's legs were contained by another sling and tied to a pole behind the cow. The cow's tail had to be contained as well.

Anyone who has never been victimized by a cow's tail, particularly when it had been marinated with cow manure has no idea what a cow's tail can and will do. Now that the cow's horns, back legs and tail have been contained, milking should commence. Just hold it! For generations on end this breed of cow had produced milk for its calf and that was it.

That had not changed even though the MCC believed to have domesticated the Creole beast from a wild animal into a Mennonite mannered milk cow. Her milk was still for her calf and nothing beyond, fore or aft. Mother gently talked to relax the cow, while father brought the calf to the cow so that she could identify it as her calf.

Trickery was necessary and a given. The cow sniffed her calf and permitted it to suck, which it did with vigor. Then father removed the calf and mother started milking, fast and furiously, at most two liters. The cow yielded little milk, but it represented a tremendous enrichment for the daily menu of a huge family. Mother was capable of fashioning all manner of miracles with milk.

Later, a second cow was added, then a third and gradually these expanded to a herd of forty to fifty cows. But for now, we milked seven to ten cows, depending on the time of year. On the basis of selective breeding, some of the cows produced five to six liters of milk per day.

This represented a source of wealth for mother since she now had sufficient milk for her children and even cream, cottage cheese, and cheese, if supplies lasted. Further, extra milk could now be sold, representing a substantial sum for mother's household budget.

When the girls, Elisabeth, Elfriede and Irene grew up, they also helped in the milking. However, the

Jacob, mother with baby Peter, Cornelius, father with Heinrich and Gerhard in front of our house in Auhagen.

realm of milking was mother's domain, until the farm was sold, at which time she was approaching sixty years. Even if she no longer did all the milking herself, she was always present, in good and bad weather. When it rained, and because all milking was invariably done outside, this was not all that great of a thrill since milking in mud and manure is not the essence of pleasure.

Upon reflecting on those times in my capacity as one of the sons, I am honestly ashamed of myself. We boys were young and strong, but the thought of helping in the milking never occurred to us. And why did we not help her in her household chores?

Mother never complained about the great amount of work. "I can" is all she said. This held true until she was ninety years old. Our parents never complained about heat or cold, the catastrophic droughts and the over-abundance of rain or when the crops lay rotting in the fields. Rather, they observed that it was too hot or too cold or dry or wet, depending on your perspective. The Chaco was simply the Chaco as it was, as it is, and will forever be. God has willed it so and prayer for rain will not change that. If you cannot live with that it is best to pack up and leave as soon as possible.

Mother and father were healthy and strong people. They were never really sick. Whereas mother used dentures, father's teeth were all in perfect condition until he was sixty and older. When father suffered a severe car accident, and no longer was as healthy and strong as formerly, mother could not really understand his decline." He always could, and now he is no longer up to it," she observed in her best Low German.

Mother's day started at the break of dawn. First she combed her hip length, full dark hair and tied it in a knot. Then she got the fire in the stove going to boil water for the morning coffee. Morning coffee sounds splendid but we had none in our settlement for years on end; it was simply too expensive. We drank mostly a coffee substitute from kefir, which was caffeine free. Still, this beverage contained valuable kefir nutrients.

Father constructed the first stove on our estate himself. He simply dug a ditch in the ground and then placed the cast iron plates (brought along from Germany) over it and it was ready to go. One end was meant for the fire while the other end was meant to disperse the smoke. This was well meant but rarely worked in practical terms since smoke conducts itself always according to the prevailing wind. Since the wind constantly changed in direction, cooking for mother was less than a pleasure. Later a stove was erected from clay bricks with a proper chimney on top, which resolved the problem of the biting smoke in the eyes.

The second item of business on the daily calendar was milking. When mother and father were finished milking, the boys were awakened, and breakfast was prepared. As soon as the entire family was assembled around the table, father conducted the morning service.

This meant a reading of scripture from the biblical calendar with all the referred to Bible verses and a detailed prayer. After father had finally concluded this sermon with an Amen, we were allowed to eat. Later, when father had difficulties with his speech, mother obviously took over this role. She read the calendar with relevant Bible references with a clear and fervent voice, then praying from her heart. Within the circle of her family, mother had no inhibitions.

After breakfast, the daily work program was divided and allotted. In summer, this meant the work on the fields. In winter, we children had to attend the village school and later high school. Thanks to mother's unceasing labor in the house and on the fields, all of the children were allowed to attend high school except the youngest two, Elfriede and Irene. When it was their turn, mother urgently needed them in the household. At father's wishes, they remained at home, although they dearly would have liked to continue their education.

When the day was over, our cattle needed looking after. Then a washing of face, hands and feet was due. Since we walked barefoot everywhere, feet washing took effort. Occasionally mother asked us to produce the towel after the washings; this towel quickly revealed the dirty party. The guilty one was quickly identified and had to re-wash his feet, this time under mother's strict watch. Then it was time for supper. Clearing of the table and washing the dishes was left to the womenfolk.

The early evening hours constituted the most pleasant part of the day. The day's work had been done. The family sat in a circle and conversed about the work of the day, or about important events of village life, or of the wider colony. Even mother was finally finished with all her work, as she sat in her easy chair to rest and relax. She could only relax when she held the youngest children on her lap since these were still much in need of their mother's love.

If one of the older children occasionally demanded a seat on mother's lap as well, such child was mercilessly teased by the older children. You are such a big one and you still want to sit on mother's lap?! Mother's lap was a privileged spot which was reserved for the young and the vulnerable. Very quickly new and young babies arrived who were next in line for mamma's lap.

Our father was highly musical. He had a melodious voice and loved to sing. He wrote in a paper just how

The growing Isaak Family.

important song was to him: singing is a gift from God which needs to be practiced. Even if Paul did not list the gift of song and music among his many spiritual gifts, this gift beyond doubt was essential. For: "Like an eagle, so soars the song, so that it happily lifts the heart to heaven and awakens in our hearts a holy desire." Where words fail or are not heard, a pious and happy song can elevate mankind to God.

There are those who claim that Luther's powerful songs contributed more to the Reformation than did his books and sermons. Not everyone is blessed with all the gifts of the Holy Spirit. However, all gifts are bestowed for service to our neighbors. And so it is with singing and music. It was father's dream that all his boys would one day become choir directors or ministers. However, only the oldest son, Gerhard, managed to become a choir director. Four of his sons, Jacob, Cornelius, Peter and Helmut became ministers of the Word, and Cornelius became a missionary while two, Jacob and Helmut, became church leaders.

When father was at home, he would often take his guitar and play beautiful songs and melodies on it. At such times, we often sang along. These evenings of song belong to the most enjoyable of our childhood memories.

Mother had the gift of immediately understanding any given situation and then deciding on the right course of action. In a large family of eleven children, things are not always peaceful even if the head of the house is a minister and a bishop.

Quarrels erupted. Jabs were exchanged and sometimes fists would fly. If no other recourse was given with older siblings, even serious biting occurred. Before the guilty party knew what was what, our mother was fully in the know, and the culprit received a hard blow with a leather slipper on the behind sufficient to guarantee good behavior and peace, for a day and more.

On the occasion of mother's ninetieth birthday, one of the children asked, "Mother, why did I get it with your slipper more often than the other siblings?" The answer came as quick as a pistol shot, "If you got more beatings with the slipper than the others, you deserved what you got." With this said, the topic was closed.

Our mother was afraid of severe thunderstorms. One day only she and one of her children were at home. Suddenly a violent thunderstorm broke out over the village. Mother hurried into the kitchen, sat down on a chair and prayed. There she found her eleven year old son, Helmut, who also was afraid of thunder. She took the boy into her arms and whispered into his ear, "I am also afraid, but God will protect us." These minutes in the safe embrace of his mother's arms is something Helmut will never forget.

Father, on the other hand, loved thunder as he loved all of nature and admired it. Whenever a real thunderstorm broke in over us, he stood under the shadow of the roof and admired nature's unbelievable fireworks. When he noticed that one of his boys, Helmut namely, was afraid of lightning and thunder, he called him to his side. When the kid tried to escape, father lifted him into his arms and explained the incredible scenery of nature to him. Helmut never again was afraid of thunder.

In addition to the three boys, Gerhard, Jacob and Cornelius who were born in Russia, Gerhard, Jacob and Cornelius, Heinrich and Peter followed in Paraguay. They were all vigorous and healthy boys. Only then was our second Elisabeth born, who from early childhood on helped our mother in the household. She was followed by two other boys, Hans and Helmut, and then two other baby girls followed; Elfriede and Irene. Then finally another boy, Harmut, was born. In all, mother gave birth to twelve healthy children over a period of 19 years. Of all the children, only little Elisabeth died in the refugee camp in Germany. Mother always had sufficient milk for all her children. A baby bottle was never to be seen in our home.

A meal menu in the Isaak home, like in all settlers' homes, was modest; oatmeal if available, or kefir porridge for breakfast. The noon meal consisted of beans or rice. Later we ate sweet potatoes or manioca fresh from the field. If we had enough flour, mother also cooked Mennonite noodles, homemade. Wrenitje, dough pockets stuffed with cottage cheese and smothered with a heavy cream sauce, were most popular. Later, when we were capable of raising our own pigs, smoked famer sausage and ham were added. It the chickens laid enough eggs, scrambled eggs were served. In summertime fritters with watermelons was the universal favorite. The evening supper consisted of leftovers from the day and kefir bread with syrup.

As the years progressed and we had bees, we frequently ate black bread with honey and drank milk as a beverage.

In autumn, mother planted a huge vegetable garden. She started the garden in late summer so that she would have the necessary seedlings to transplant. These included cabbage and kohlrabi, radishes and tomatoes, rutabagas and red beets, onions and garlic. If the winters were not too dry, and the frost did not burn the plants, we generally had a good crop. Onions and garlic were dried and braided into long garlands and hung in the pantry. It was mother's intention to harvest sufficient onions so that they would last till next winter. She, then, would not have to buy any so that she could save money from a sparse budget. All of us children worked in the garden. The planting of onions was a chore, since they had to be planted in exactly the same given distance from the next set. Obviously hoeing the garden was the next step of constant work activity.

The sorrel (zuromp) bloomed exactly at Easter time. When the red caps were fully grown, they were harvested. The red fruit meat was dried in the sun and kept for months on end. Sorrel reds could also be stamped into bottles and sealed airtight with a cork or bee's wax and used for the making of jam or crumble cake.

These same sorrel bushes became the favorite hunting areas for our boys, who, armed with slingshots, shot partridges, which favored the sorrel seeds. Mother's face beamed when the boys appeared with a partridge, since she could then boil a highly nutritious soup from it or cook a delicious roast.

Mother was also most adept in the orchard. We had grapefruit, oranges, lemons, mandarins, pomegranates and guavas. Guavas were converted into delicious jams which lasted all season.

We had already established a huge orchard in Auhagen. In Blumenort, we greatly expanded our orchard holdings. When the orchard was fully planted and matured with a fine production, the great drought of 1948 set in. We did not have a single drop of rain for eight months. Everything not native to the Chaco perished. Only the barbed Chaco bush survived, even though we much wanted it burned to extinction. Barely one quarter of our orchard survived. Under normal circumstances with sufficient moisture we had a surplus of oranges, grapefruits, mandarins, lemons and guavas.

In autumn, when nights were cool, we butchered pigs for winter. Every last bit of the pig was utilized. Even the pig bristles were used as stuffing for the horses' harnesses and collars. We made cracklings, lard, ham, smoked and liver sausage. Hog lard was used for frying and baking. To get all the desired fat, pigs had to be well fed and fattened.

In autumn, we also made syrup from sugar cane. The juice was squeezed out of the reeds and then reduced by cooking for hours on end in a flat container, to evaporate all the water. When the cane was then reduced to a stiff gel it was canned for the winter. Mother saw to it that the pantry was well stocked for our huge family.

Visitors from far and near came and went. Whenever father was in Filadelfia, and prominent people like Orie Miller, Harold S. Bender or J. J. Thiessen came visiting to the Chaco, they generally intended to speak to father at length and in detail and he brought them home with him. It was a given that the best from kitchen and pantry were served to the guests. Generally this meant very nutritious beans, sweet potatoes and manioca or whatever else was available in the garden.

Irene remembers an experience of all this when she was a young child. Waffles with excellent pudding were a top culinary priority in the Isaak family. As a small girl, she had persuaded mother to make waffles with pudding for lunch the next day. So mother planned to keep sufficient milk in reserve the next morning and prepared the pudding right away, while it was still cool outside. With the eager help of her little daughter, this was done. At 11 a. m. the thin dough with numerous eggs was mixed. The waffle iron was cleaned and placed on the heat of the kitchen stove and the baking of waffles commenced. And then, mercy me! Just as the waffles were done, father appeared on the yard with the buggy bearing four visitors.

They were hungry and could hardly believe their good fortune at waffles and pudding being served. Guests and visitors were always served first, with children being next in line; such was the unwritten rule, carved in stone. And so it was as father and his visitors sat down at the table, who appeared to be ravenous. When they were finished eating, not a trace of waffles or pudding was left. Irene stood looking inside from a crack in the widow and reported to her hungry siblings: "They have eaten every scrap!" In the meantime, mother had cooked a large pot of beans for the children as a meager substitute. Tears flowed. Mother embraced Irene who had helped her so excitedly and whispered in her ear, "I will again make waffles and pudding tomorrow and just for the two of us." She kept her word.

For Irene, mother was not only the best of mothers but also her best friend. She could entrust her with all her joys and sorrows because she knew that mother would keep it all to herself. In general, our parents took more time for the youngest ones with this being appreciated by both parties. Since father now owned a vw, he was able to spend more evening time with the family. This led to a more intimate relationship with the three youngest children; such had obviously not been possible with the larger family.

Since father was a man of many and wide interests and curious about life, he became aware of the apiary trade. A fellow settler in a neighboring village had successfully experimented with honey bees. Now the Isaaks also procured a series of bee hives.

When Hans, number eight in the Isaak line, stated that he had had enough of high school, he was allowed to remain at home. Helmut profited from that decision since he could now attend high school without interruption. To this day, Helmut is grateful to Hans for this decision.

High School, Nursing School, Bible School and Teacher Training Schools were all financed from the proceeds of the farm. Anyone of us who intended to seek education beyond these institutions, was on his own in financing such venture. If students intended to attend the Biblical Seminary in Montevideo, the respective churches financed these studies. However, this arrangement did not apply to the Isaak children.

They had to look after their own means and finances. Father would not think of using his influence in church for preferential treatment for his children. Father received $100.00 for Helmut from the First Mennonite Church in Saskatoon, Saskatchewan, Canada, and paid an additional equal sum out of his own pocket. With this money in pocket, Helmut was able to assume his studies in Montevideo, and, with much additional part-time work, after five years he managed to complete his studies there successfully.

Since the older brothers were in school or learning a trade, Hans was now responsible for all the work on the fields. Since father was unable to pay him for his selfless work, he was allowed to take over the apiary. He was allowed to produce as much honey as he wanted to, and as the bees could produce. The only condition was that he had to supply the entire household with as much honey as required and free of charge. This was a considerable amount, since the Isaaks were not modest in honey intake. Despite this, Hans managed to sell honey by the ton in good years.

Helmut, who assisted him all summer long, received not a penny for his labors. And so Helmut very early learned that learning and studying, while immensely interesting, indeed fascinating, had little to do with the making of money. This is particularly true of the arts and studies therein.

Hans is the one who worked for father for the longest without pay. His older brothers and also his sisters were allowed to leave home at sixteen, seventeen or eighteen in order to learn a trade or a profession.

Hans remained at home and ran the entire operation till he was 25 when he was finally able to buy the farm from father on installments. Although Hans had worked unselfishly and pro bono for the entire family for years on end, he had to pay the full price for the farm. One of the brothers, Helmut, at

Ox hitched to a cultivator.

the time advised his father to gift Hans the farm or to sell it to him at a reduced rate in consideration that Hans had worked for it and maintained it over so many years and without pay.

This was not possible. Father was still not adequately paid for his work and depended on an income from the farm. In addition, the vw devoured huge amounts of money. And so Hans did not only have to pay the full amount for the farm, but father also kept the 50 head of cattle which Hans, his wife Hilda, and their two daughters had looked after free of charge for years on end. The two youngest sisters worked at home without pay until they married. Hartmut also was allowed to attend high school and the Teacher Training Institute. It was his intention to study chemistry in Asuncion. Nothing came of it. Father needed an additional income. And so, Hartmut worked as a watchmaker with the proceeds landing in father's pocket, to keep the expensive vw afloat.

When springtime arrived, father, or mother, or sometimes both sat down with the boys to plan the seeding. Then the boys were allowed to suggest where the cotton, the kefir, peanuts, beans and watermelons should be planted. Father or mother occasionally made other suggestions and these were discussed and resolved. And so, the boys were included in planning the work in the fields. This resulted in such work being much more interesting since they were included in the responsibilities of the operation.

During the first years, mother always came out to the field. While father, together with a neighbor's help, labored with the oxen in plowing furrow after furrow, mother strewed the seed on the ground. They planted beans, cotton, kefir and peanuts. Then the Isaaks, like the Auhageners, learned to cultivate sweet potatoes and manioca as well; later they even learned to eat them. In truth, they never liked them.

We children were constantly reminded just how wonderful, indeed incredibly delicious, potatoes tasted. When we finally got to eat them, we found them tasteless. We much preferred sweet potatoes and manioca and do so to this day. We planted watermelons and other melons as well. When the many plants then sprouted and grew, hoeing was upon us!

Mother invariably also got involved in this work. She had her youngest child on her arm and made for the field. Then the baby was placed on a blanket in the shade of a tree and the work commenced. Everyone got involved in picking cotton. When the fields were small, we managed on our own but in time as the fields grew we hired labor.

As children, we never received any pocket money and later father occasionally asked for forgiveness for not doing so. The fathers of our friends, who were always at home and were not honorary minister or church leaders, could afford to pay their children a meager sum in pocket money. These could then afford to indulge their wishes of the hearts, like buy an ice-cream on a once weekly run to Filadelfia . We Isaak children were left to dream of such unheard of luxuries. Once a year, the Isaak children were given a chance to come to money, and this was at the cotton harvest when we were paid for every kilo of picked cotton on par with what the hired hands received. We worked very hard. Come evenings, the cotton was weighed and the weights registered. After the harvest we received the money due, with which we had to make do until the next harvest in a year's time.

During the years of settlement, father always had a very hard time with the oxen. Mornings, when it was cool, they pulled gladly and evenly, leaving straight furrows in their slow wake. However, in the heat of the day, it was difficult to restrain them. They were used to resting in the shade when it was hot and when they had had their fill of pulling plows, they simply took off for the shade of a tree for more comfortable quarters dragging everything behind them. When father then became angry or discouraged, mother placed a comforting arm on his shoulder. “Let them rest. In the cool of the evening we will catch up for labor lost.”

When the family came home from the fields, the fire in the stove had to be started. Beans were cooked for lunch and eaten with good appetite. If the boys occasionally complained the word was: “You don’t have to eat them, but that’s all you’re getting.” Ripe watermelons provided an excellent dessert.

However, watermelons were served only after the beans had been eaten. Soon people knew: at the Isaak table you eat what is provided and no fussing at the table.

The later wives of these boys came to appreciate this. “My husband will eat any- and everything I bring to the table”, was the word.

The Auhageners had very quickly recognized father’s special gifts. He was peaceful, stuck to the subject at hand and he was discreet. People could confide in him, knowing that he would never disclose confidentialities. Further, he was absolutely reliable. Also, he was the best mediator in the village, whenever a quarrel broke out. And so it was not long before Jacob Isaak was chosen as the distributor of MCC packages of food.

This was always a touchy business. Since the rations were distributed on the basis of persons to a family, and families with adults only received no more than families with children, these believed that they were receiving the shorter end of the food stick. It was father’s task to distrubute the food evenly amongst all the families. The distributions transpired fairly and peacefully with only one family getting too little and this was his own. Occasionally mother reminded him of this, but he replied, “You know that others need it more than we. We will make do.”

Our older siblings remember that father or mother during the meals often said, “I am not hungry today. You just eat everything there is.” And that is exactly what happened. Young, growing boys are always ravenous. However, the younger boys also remember that occasionally they heard their mother weep during the night.

The colony community soon became aware of our father. When, at one of the many meetings things became boisterous, father suggested that peace and reflection be allowed to prevail. People noticed this and asked who this young man was. In short order father was asked to assume some position, which demanded much voluntary work. Father thanked them, saying, “I will not be your pack donkey.”

That remark probably came off as arrogant. However, father knew that the call of his Lord and Savior would come to him sooner than later. Then he would not be able to refuse. For this Lord and Master he would not only be a pack donkey, but also a servant and a slave. Such services are not paid in clanging coinage or public titles but with blessings and inner joy in the service of your neighbor. And when the faithfulness of the servant is tried, the bearing of the cross is added for extra measure.

During the village meetings, difficult arguments sometimes took place. On one occasion a nasty exchange of words ensued between father and his neighbor Johann Boldt. This dispute was not resolved and both went home. Our father could not sleep that night. Early the next morning, he set out for the neighbor's yard to ask forgiveness. Halfway there, he met Boldt who came his way to likewise ask forgiveness. That quarrel was quickly laid to rest.

Mennonite men smoking in Russia was a given. Our father also smoked during the early years in the Chaco. One day, father's tobacco ran out and he walked over to a neighbor to borrow some. However, en route it occurred to him how childish and selfish his habit was. The family has barely enough to eat and here he is puffing away the last of his money on tobacco. He turned around on the spot and never smoked again.

A second version of this episode runs like this: In the eyes of the Mennonite Brethren, smoking was a sin and they let the General Conference Mennonites know that smokers and their church, for that matter, would land in hell. One day, when the G.C. ministers rolled their cigarettes, they talked about it and decided if the loving Brethren take such strong offence at smoking we might just as well put an end to it. They agreed to stop smoking.

Of course, there were also M.B.'s who smoked, but they did this secretly behind the barn or in a secret biffy where they could not be surprised. Since we children were in the know, as children invariably are, we called these smokers "Biffy Puffers." Obviously there were G.C.'s who smoked secretly as well.

What many probably did not know, is that our father was an excellent shot and hunter. He never spoke in our company of his marksmanship. Later, when our pantry was well stocked, father never hunted and the younger Isaak children never saw him with a gun. In earlier times in the Chaco when food was rare, father invariably hunted for fresh meat for our family and our neighbors as well.

Father's friend Peter Fast, who resided in Asuncion, stored all his guns with father for safe-keeping, and father had free use of them. And so it happened, that in the early years when our pantry was bare, father would go hunting. Invariably he shot a deer, a wild boar or a fat drake or duck. Wild boar was our favorite wild game and our many neighbor's as well.

To supply the village with beef was a further occasion for father to demonstrate his marksmanship. The MCC had bought virtually entire herds of wild cattle for the settlers in the Casado area. These herds of cattle were wild and grazed in the vicinity of our villages.

When the weekly slaughtering was due, the village animals were herded into the village corral. There were no good riding horses available at the time and the young village boys were not yet handy with lassos. To walk among relatively wild animals was dangerous in the extreme because the cattle had very long horns on either side of the head, and so it was a precarious business to isolate the animal for slaughter. The resolution of the problem was simple. The village mayor went to father handing him a military rifle and said, "Jake, now it's your turn." Then my father raised a steady gun, a steadier eye and a deadly bullet and shot the animal of choice. Father always met their expectations; he never missed.

One day the boys came running to the house excitedly. “Father, there are wild boar at our watering hole!” This drink was more than two hundred meters distance from our house. Father went for the rifle, placed it on a fence post, aimed and fired and a big boar was fit for the skillet and this story. Mother was most happy for nothing tasted better than a roast of wild boar. Our neighbors likewise never declined a juicy roast of wild boar ham or venison.

Another hunting story that also refuses to die to this day goes like this. In spring, when the great rains came, the natural pools and ponds around the village were filled with water. With the rain, water birds arrived. Ducks were among these birds. Father was particularly interested in the large black drakes with their white wings. These male species weighed more than six pounds and were a delicacy of rare order. Our mother prepared them with great care and rendered them into a favorite on the Isaak menu.

With this in mind father spanned the horizon with a watchful eye, ever on the lookout for ducks landing in ponds, while working the fields. After work, he would then make his way on a hunting mission. And sure enough, a drake was on his way. However, the direction and intent of landing was wrong. Instead of the drake landing on the next pond, it headed for a neighbor’s giant bottle tree, a few farmyards down and landed.

Father reflected. Then he called his oldest boy and handed the reins over to him; it was plowing time. Since father did not have his rifle handy, he walked over to the neighbor and requested loan of a shotgun. The neighbor handed it over gladly, savoring a potential roast of duck. After thanking him, father made for that yard and with careful aim, knocked the drake out of the tree. Then father again expressed his thanks and was about to leave with the fat drake when the neighbor interjected.

He believed he could have shot the drake just as well himself. "Of course," answered father, "but you had no idea where the drake was roosting." That drake provided a huge and delicious meal for the entire family but also provided wonderful down for the pillows of the family. A series of ducks, so hunted, in time filled every pillow of our family.

The boys also went hunting wild pigeons and partridges with slingshots and their hope was to shoot a wild duck as well. The boys were particularly eager to hunt when father was not around. When the pantry was bare, our mother gave in to their pleas and allowed them to hunt when the hoeing was done and the cotton picked, but had them promise that they would bring home their booty.

Obviously the boys, whose imagination matched their hunting ambitions, knew a thing or two about shooting a bird or a wild piglet and then roasting it on a spit in the middle of a contained bush camp fire. Since such meals were secret and not shared, father did not take kindly to these adventures and after administering a tongue lashing without a Bible verse, removed all traces of dust from their pants by a sturdy hand.

When the boys were older, they were disinclined to always follow mother's orders. Our father was gone on some mission and the cotton had to be transported to Filadefia for sale. To load the cotton on a wagon and to transport it to Filadelfia to the cotton gin was no problem. However, mother was of mixed emotions when she realized which horses her boy had hitched to the wagon.

He had not chosen the passive and proven draft horses which were always hitched up for such work. Her son had hitched young, unruly and half-broken horses to the cotton wagon. These were known to bolt whenever they were startled or when they encountered the unfamiliar.

Mother advised her son to hitch the more sedate horses to the wagon. He responded, "I will manage to control them well." Finally mother gave in. The load was not yet around the first corner when the horses bolted. They galloped wildly through the village, stampeding down the road. The young driver lost control over the horses.

When he attempted to guide them towards the village fence, the wheels crashed into a fence post and the wagon was torn apart. The horses were attached to each other only by the wagon-tree, which broke as they bolted. Finally a neighbor managed to catch them and he brought them home. Then the various wagon parts strewn and scattered all over were collected and pieced together.

Finally, the cotton widely dispersed was gathered in and delivered to Filadelfia the next day. Our brother was spared injury. However, his pride has sustained a hard blow and a bump. This did not much improve when our father returned. Our brother chose to listen to mother's counsel as of that day.

Once the sun set, kerosene lamps were lit. By their meager light the final housework was done, while reading could also be done close to the lamps. One evening, mother quickly walked around the corner to retrieve a broom she had leaned against a far wall. It was pitch black. While reaching for the broom a great, sudden and nameless fear seized her. Without moving an inch, she called for her children. When they approached with a flashlight they saw a large, fuming adder ready to strike, if anyone dared approach. The boys dispatched this snake on the spot and in an instant. When mother then realized in what imminent mortal danger she had been, she had to sit down and compose herself.

There were poisonous snakes all over the Chaco. As far as I know no one during the years of settlement was ever bitten fatally by a rattle snake, a viper, an adder or a corral snake.

After the summer was over, and my parents had completed the harvest, father and mother built their first house. Father carried the raw timber home on his shoulders and fashioned windows and door frames from it. The walls were constructed with adobe bricks, air-dried. The roof was thatched with reeds. These kept the house dry but also cool in summer and warm in the winter. The house was roomy with two large, comfortable rooms. Both were used

Peanuts, harvested by hand.

Adobe walls plastered with clay and finely chopped bitter grass which provided protection against sun and rain.

as bedrooms and as living quarters. The walls were plastered with clay both in and outside. Since clay cracks readily, bitter grass was finely chopped and mixed into the clay. This represented an excellent protection for the walls, particularly where they are exposed to the rain and the sun. Out of the very fine and white ash from burned quebracho wood, a kind of white paint is made which gives the whole house an attractive, off-white appearance.

Mother continued to cook underneath the overhang of the roof. Father laid the bricks for a sturdy stove and fashioned a proper chimney at the end. For baking purposes, a proper bake oven was constructed in which tasty bread, delicious buns, crumble cake or sorrel tortes were baked.

The interior furnishings were also improved. Cross saws produced boards for doors and window frames. From now on our family was protected from wild thunder storms, northern breezes, or the ice-cold southerly Chaco winds as was the case in the tent villages. Slowly mother felt like a real house and farmer's wife, who had something to offer her ever growing family. There was no window screening available yet. To protect the family from the bothersome mosquito plagues during the rainy season, the usual mosquiteros provided the necessary protection.

The dry winter months were utilized to expand the seeding acreage. On the open camps, quebracho and urundey trees mostly grow. These had to be chopped down, then removed together with their roots up to a depth of half a meter. To that end,

A bake oven in which mother baked delicious bread, crumble cake, buns and other goods.

the roots are initially exposed by spade and then chopped off. When the giant, heavy tree finally falls, it has to be cleaned up. To accomplish this it is burned, a most time consuming process since Chaco hardwood burns very slowly. In the burning of wood, mother was the most effective, since she knew the workings of fire like no one else.

The boys also enjoyed playing with fire especially when sparks were flying all around. Since forest fires do not exist in the Chaco because the Chaco bush simply refuses to burn, anyone can play with fire to their heart's content. The occasional burn teaches old but mostly the young to be careful when playing with fire.

In the morning the entire family set out to clear the bush. Father swung a mighty axe while mother and children set fire to the fallen trees. If things went well, a mighty tree per day could be brought to fall and burned. If, however, the rains of spring appeared and plowing is urgent, a quicker method is brought into play. Right next to the heavy tree trunk a ditch was dug in the soft earth and the trunk was simply rolled into it and buried. If the ditch was not dug deep enough, the plow would snag it and be damaged. This had to be avoided at all cost. Gradually, in this way our fields increased year to year.

When father was chosen minister of the Word in 1932, mother was not surprised. She had discussed this possibility on numerous occasions. However, mother also knew that father would need to spend more and more time at work in that capacity. He received no payment for his work. Already in Russia, ministers were not paid and the same now held true for the Chaco. Mother was a strong and resilient woman, who approached all work with a happy and courageous disposition. Together with her children, she would have to assume the main responsibility in managing the economics of the farm. She was everywhere: in the household, on the yard and on the fields. In addition to all this work, she gave birth to an additional eight children in the Chaco, raising a healthy family and father helping where and whenever he could.

However, church work was the main priority. He had vowed to do this before God and he kept his word. The promised blessing did not come by way of material goods, but in nine healthy children who carried out the work in the household and on the fields as a matter of course. All of the children developed into healthy, strong and good people.

During the first years in the Chaco father fought many inner battles. God had led him and his family out of Russia and into the Chaco. Here they were free from all oppression, exploitation and subordination by political rulers. But real freedom demands content, and has to have an aim and a future; in short, freedom demands essence.

Freedom needs a material base in order to develop. With regards to aim and purpose of this newly found freedom in the Chaco, discussions transpired already in the beginning years in the Chaco. God had sent them to the Chaco so that they could live their faith in peace. They also very early and clearly understood that such peace meant a great responsibility in evangelizing the Indians.

In Russia Mennonites had neglected to evangelize the Natives. In fact, in the privileges extended to them, they had promised not to evangelize the Orthodox Russians. There were those who regarded the downfall of the Mennonite colonies in Russia as punishment from God for such neglect. This was not to be repeated in the Chaco. For this reason, during the beginning years in the Chaco a missionary society called "Light for the Indians" was founded.

And yet, was a future at all to be realized in this land without roads, inhospitable and undeveloped? Would they not have to admit after a few years that there was simply no future of any kind in the Chaco? Would they not simply disintegrate? The question as to whether a sound existence could be realized in the Chaco at all found answer only after decades of hard work and the response was a simple but resounding "Yes, indeed!"

Were there not other countries or other possibilities where he could have provided a respectable living for his family? Permission for them to stay in Germany had been granted. However, neither father nor mother were ever German citizens. When they were later offered German passports, they declined them. Russia had been their home and Canada was meant to be their new home. However, Canada refused them entry and so they now had to try to make a new home in the inhospitable Chaco.

Father struggled with God. Did his vow apply to this hopeless wilderness? Should he also sacrifice the well-being of his beloved Elisabeth and his many children? Where was the blessing God had promised him? Father had made great plans for his life. He intended to attend university and gain laurels as an academic. But God, or, rather the Communist Party, had destroyed these plans. Also, his plan to migrate to America via Batum did not materialize.

Then he became acquainted with Elisabeth Hildebrandt and they married. Yet again, a highly promising future emerged. More land could be acquired. The farm could be expanded. However, Communism torpedoed these aspirations. Good Brethren of Mennonite faith from North America took them, the homeless and stateless, to the hopeless wilderness of the Gran Chaco.

In 1931, when a group of Mennonite settlers cast about for an alternative in East Paraguay, the MCC did everything in its power to prevent them from re-settling. They were to remain in this hopeless, inhospitable Chaco. Finally, father gave up all hope, progress and material security. When he finally managed to unconditionally submit to God, he was blessed. Only then did the Chaco become his promised land, which he had to make fertile through hard work with ax, spade and plow. The Chaco remained the promised land for father and mother till the end of their days. Through their determined labor, they contributed to the Chaco becoming a veritable Paradise for the next generations, provided that sufficient rain fell.

All this did not transpire without new struggles. When father in 1948 traveled to the Mennonite World Conference as the representative of the Fernheim Colony, to Goshen and Newton, Kansas, he also traveled through all of Canada. He was particularly impressed with the Fraser Valley of British Columbia, Canada. Father had many friends and relatives in the USA and Canada, who would have facilitated a settlement there for him and his large family.

But he knew that neither the USA nor Canada were the promised lands for him and his family. His land was meant to be the infamous Chaco, Paraguay. When his sons later migrated to Brazil, Canada and Germany, he always advised against such moves. He let them have their will, but insisted that it was possible to realize a secure economic life in the inhospitable Chaco. Was this not self-evident?

When in 1948 he finally returned home from North America, locusts had destroyed our every field. Not only that, the catastrophic drought had destroyed most of his beloved fruit trees. Cotton and kefir could be re-planted and harvested. The fruit trees, on the other hand, took years to again bear fruit.

When one of his sons asked him in 1980, whether migrating to Canada had not been a temptation, he freely admitted it. However, had God not blessed him and his Lisa in this land after years of hard labor and many deprivations with all material goods, so that they were well looked after in their old age?

Is not all of this earth God's creation and therewith the promised land? Does not God's proclamation, "Your faith will sustain you, and you will prevail" apply everywhere where His children attempt to eke out an existence?

CHAPTER III
Pack Donkey of the Lord on the Road to Serenity.

THE REFUGEES, who managed to leave Russia in 1929, came from various colonies and from three different church affiliations: the Mennonite Church (also called the Conference), the Evangelical Mennonite Brethren Church (EMB) and the Mennonite Brethren Church (MB). In the villages, they all lived interspersed, since in the compilations of the village communities, nor in the refugee camps in Germany, deliberately no attention was paid to church membership.

Prof. B. Unruh advised all refugees, while they were still in German refugee camps, to forget all their differences of the past and for all to start afresh as one church voice when settling in Paraguay. And while he constantly reminded of such unity forthwith, his admonitions were of no avail. The settlers had barely arrived on their new land, when the individual church congregations were again immediately organized in accordance with original membership patterns in Russia. The M.B's wanted to be M.B.'s again, the EMB's were again the EMB's and the Conference chose to be the Mennonite Conference. As a final resort, they did manage to organize as the Fernheim Mennonite Conference.

At the outset, this group called itself the Conference of Mennonite Congregations. Since the term Conference had retained a bitter aftertaste of mediocrity from the past, it soon was re-baptized as the Fernheim Mennonite Conference. From Russia, the term Conference was associated with the unconverted, superficial and those not properly baptized. It was above all the Brethren who made this an object of stickler point for years to come.

When the Auhageners arrived at their site of settlement, the three mentioned Mennonite churches were already in place. Father and mother were both members since 1920 of the Mennonite Conference based on baptism in Russia of their faith in Jesus Christ. It was this church, the Mennonite Conference, which very soon called father into the ministry. Since father himself describes the condition of this congregation in his inaugural sermon in 1934 held in the Auhagen School, we best let him have his say in the matter.

THE REASON FOR SPEAKING
2. Corinthians: 4:13-14

Every person created in the image of God goes his own, individual way. God the Lord, however, who created man out of a clod of earth, and who blew into him the living breath and gave him a free will, sometimes has to wait long before this creation finds its way back to Him. Also, most often this creature wants to be more clever than his maker. How wondrously did God create all things. He had planned for man a wonderful life in His garden.

However this wondrously gifted man allowed himself to be misled by the snake, the devil, by the compelling question, "Would you not like to be like God?" This artful flattering struck the very heart of our first parents. We can, in fact, be like God. Initially they resisted this appeal, Did God not say? But the snake quickly knew how to overcome this resistance. The idea of being like God overrode all such reservations. Adam and Eve decided to act against God's command. They did not want anyone to be superior to them and broke God's command. My dear ones, here assembled, the sin of Adam and Eve was their great fall. If we now ask, if matters today are different, we have to answer, that people today also suffer from the same sin. Today, also, man wants to be like God, or even to play God himself. Also today man resists God's command.

"We are all sinners and lack the honor, we are meant to have before God," the Apostle Paul wrote. Only after the words of Jesus find fulfillment in our heart, "Unless you are born again," resistance against God's will stops. Only then is the original, God-willed relationship to Him again given. Only then does the created being become available to the Creator's will. However, even for us as born-again children of God, the battle of temptation to be like God never stops. Every child of God knows about this battle and the wrestling involved. And so do I! How long does it take, and how many inner battles have to be fought before man finally walks the path of salvation? The answer is: Until man accepts the crucified Son of God and the only savior there is, Jesus Christ and believes in Him. How much love and patience must God invest in us? How difficult it is for mankind to finally answer from an honest heart, "I believe!" I believe that Jesus Christ the Son of God is also my Savior. My dear ones here assembled, I have experienced exactly this and so have many of you.

When I started attending Youth Instruction at twenty years of age in Lichtenau, it became clear to me that I had to embark on a different life. I had to reverse my course from the walk of sin. I, too, had to be converted if I intended to inherit eternal life. During those instructions, the way to salvation was clearly revealed to me. But I did not manage to grasp it. Then, in the night of May 11, 1920 and only after dreadful inner struggles, I was finally able to obtain the certainty that my sins had been forgiven. Since that night, I also know how difficult it is to state truthfully, "I believe!" Only after an inner voice told me, "All you have to do is to believe it," was I able to grasp the connection and find inner peace.

Based on this faith, I was baptized and based on this faith I take and make the step today. Based on this faith, I have accepted your call and God's call and have given affirmative response to this great and heavy responsibility which I now assume.

"I believe, therefore have I spoken," says the Psalmist in Psalm 116. The Apostle Paul likewise refers to his faith as the basis of speaking, preaching, "And since we believe, we also speak." This is the only reason I stand before you today and speak. I know full well that I am but a humble servant and a ponderous speaker. Also I know what it takes to formulate a cohesive sermon.

Dearly beloved, here assembled: I have to tell you today how difficult it was for me to consent to become your minister. I hesitated for a long while before I agreed to assume the work. I have managed to find peace within, therefore I stand before you today. After all, I had made a vow to God that I would serve Him if He would deliver me and my family out of Russia.

After we arrived in Germany through God's grace, I often pondered how I could honor the vow I made. While we were yet in Mőlln at the train station, Jacob K. Janzen called me, "If and when they choose you to be a minister, then do not refuse." I cannot say how I felt at that time. I know that if I could have remained behind, I would have done so. An inner voice informed me that things would come to this. However, everything within me resisted this call. I felt unworthy and incompetent to assume this load.

After we arrived here in Auhagen, I participated in a congregational meeting of the Mennonite Conference Church. There was much work to be done. And yet, where were the workers? After a few weeks, an election of ministers transpired and I was elected. However, I hesitated in my decision to accept. I felt like Moses, "I lack the talent to speak." Or like Isaiah, "Who am I, Lord, that I shall go and preach? Woe unto me, for I have unclean lips."

It was at a prayer meeting that I found answer to every question, "I believe and therefore I will speak." Now my eyes were opened and I knew what to say, namely my faith in Jesus Christ, our Lord and Savior. Then I commenced in humility to preach.

Then your call for ordination arrived. And again, my inner struggle was great. I knew about the great damages inflicted by ourselves and within our church to the church itself. I knew about the lukewarm, cold and indifferent conduct of many members in our congregation. The life of many members bore no connection with the teachings of Christ, that much was obvious. But it also became clear to me that God had led me explicitly to this church to honor my vow. I have to speak candidly to you today. I have to tell you what moved my heart. Would not sooner or later exactly that happen to our church what once happened to Israel when Jesus confronted them with these words, "The Kingdom of God will be taken from you." These words by Jesus went into fulfillment, unfortunately, in shortest order. And what was the exact reason for Israel's disobedience and unfaithfulness?

Dear congregation, are we not today on the very same path if we look around us in all honesty? Where are we today in matters of discipleship? Remember our promises which we made when we stood at the border of freedom when leaving Russia. Did we not then promise to be faithful servants and followers of Jesus Christ? Or when typhoid rampaged among us and we made every promise to God to restore us at that time? Or the youth of our church; did you not, when accepting Jesus as your Lord and Savior a few months ago, promise to follow Him? And where are you today? Can we in good conscience appear before God or would we fail? If our testimony were empty words at our baptism, then we have betrayed not only our members but even ourselves.

Dear congregation, let us be mindful and wakeful. Today is the day of grace. Today is the day that we take seriously the discipleship of Jesus Christ. Of what use is a beautiful dress if the bearer is dead? Of what use is the name Mennonite if we do not live our faith?

I believe and therefore I speak. I know that He, who awakened Jesus from the dead, will also lead us through death and to eternal life. Jesus Christ, yesterday, today and in all eternity. That is the content of my sermon and shall remain so for all time. We can become redeemed only in Him and through Him.

Dear Congregation: Pray for me, and a steadfast faith. Pray that I may have strength, joy and courage and that I may preach to you the faith of Jesus Christ faithfully and genuinely and in practice. Amen!

When our parents joined the Fernheim Mennonite Conference, they knew only too well the prejudices of the other two churches. However, they also knew that they were not subordinate to the judgment and decree of these cantankerous "fellows" but that they were responsible only to God, their Lord and Judge. It is before this Judge who knows the hearts of all mankind, that no one can pass on the basis of his conversion and baptism, and not even on the strength of a purely lived life but only on God's infinite grace, as revealed in Jesus Christ. However, as justified sinners, we are children of God as long as we walk in weakness and impurity on the path of discipleship.

In his inaugural sermon, father spoke candidly about his inner battles and his imperfections. He knew his weaknesses all too well. He also knew that in the future new temptations and afflictions would continue to assail him. But he also knew from personal experience, that Jesus Christ had died for him, and that His power became mighty in the weak. When the inner voice whispered to him during his wrestling "All you have to do is to believe" this applied to yet another matter. Father was gifted, strong and proud. He wanted to do things on his own, and in his own way. Faith for him meant that he had to humble himself before God. He had to realize that he was a sinful man and that he would never make it on his strength alone. This meant that he would have to live with all his strengths and weaknesses. He, also, had to learn and confess that in the final analysis things come down to grace alone.

Even he as minister and later bishop of his church, was still vulnerable to temptations and he, too, still made mistakes and if he daily depended on his salvation exclusively on the infinite love and grace of God in Jesus Christ, then who was he to judge other people? Was a church free of sin possible at all? Or was the church of Jesus Christ, from the time of the apostles, not a community of those who heard and accepted the call into discipleship and now follow Christ with all their imperfections?

This awareness humbled father and made him accessible and tolerant towards others. God had appointed him to be not the judge of his congregation but its shepherd and teacher. As such, it was his duty to care for the weak, the wounded, and the lost.

In a talk "The Shepherd According to Scripture", father develops this very thought. Already in the Old Testament, the great leaders and prophets of Israel like Moses, Isaiah, Ezekiel, and others are termed the shepherds of the people of God. According to Ephesians 4:11 some of the gifts of the spirit are the shepherds of the church. Jesus talks of himself as being the good shepherd, who seeks the lost sheep in order to rescue it. If neighboring churches constantly harped on the shortcomings of the Mennonite Conference, father very calmly responded, "Unfortunately we know all that full well, but we are working on it!" Just like Jesus seeks the lost sheep to bring it back into the fold, we follow suit. Further, it is the duty of the shepherd to feed his flock. This means supplying them everything to enable a healthy life. He has to protect his flock from internal and external dangers. In this very context, father points to the dangers of political streams of the day which represent a constant danger to the church. "Our past experience has taught us this lesson. They are the wolves in sheep's clothing." Therefore the shepherd must constantly watch and pray in order to properly evaluate the spirits. The admonition of John the Apostle "Try the spirits" will apply ever more as we progress.

Already on May 24, 1931, the first baptism was celebrated in the Mennonite Conference Church in Kleefeld. All candidates were required to participate in preparatory Youth and Catechism classes. They were baptized on their personal testimony in their belief in Jesus Christ as taught in the New Testament. Biblical faith, however, always means obedience. In father's inaugural sermon he states that faith without obedience is no faith at all. For father, faith became genuine faith only when it was lived unconditionally.

In Russia the influence of Pietism had been a major factor in the birth of the Mennonite Brethren Church with personal salvation becoming ever more a dominant demand. Just as in the other churches, baptismal candidates later had to testify to a personal conversion experience before the Mennonite Conference Congregation. This represents an obvious shift in accent. It is no longer enough for the candidate to confess faith, but such candidate was also required to tell the story of just how he had arrived at that faith. The How and When of conversion became constantly more important in the Fernheim Mennonite Conference as well. Conversion and faith were not mutually exclusive if conversion really led to true faith and unconditional obedience. However, it is not the How and When of the conversion which represents salvation, but the clear decision for discipleship of Jesus Christ in daily life, meaning faith and obedience.

Regarding the How and When of conversion, the form of conversion as influenced by the Baptists became a major concern. For the Mennonite Brethren, dating back to Russia, only baptism by immersion was valid. Other forms of baptism were not respected, or accepted. If, for whatever reason, a member of the Mennonite Conference intended to become a member of the Mennonite Brethren, a re-baptism was mandatory. The main reasons for this stipulation were the so-called mixed marriages. Until the time the Mennonite Brethren accepted the sprinkling form of baptism, this one-sided emphasis on baptism caused unspeakable amounts of heartache and tensions.

Church services were conducted under the shade of trees during the first years, then in private homes and, finally in the village schools. Since all three church affiliations were represented in most villages, they held services in common. The exception was the Church Sunday which later was held once monthly. On this given Sunday, each congregation conducted its own service. On other Sundays father preached to all three church affiliations.

Father's testimony of his conversion, his faith and his unconditional obedience to Jesus Christ finally convinced even the extreme members of the Mennonite Brethren Church that he was right with God. Also, the content of his sermons was convincing, even though his emphasis on faith as unconditional obedience and the unconditional discipleship was too much for some of them. However, the form and the rite of his baptism, namely baptism by sprinkling, was a matter which many found lacking.

This matter went so far that word went out to the effect, that if Uncle Isaak were only properly baptized again, he would qualify for ministerial material of the Mennonite Brethren Church. This was yet another example of form being ranked higher than faith and the testimony of discipleship. The members of the Mennonite Brethren Church were convinced that: If you were not properly saved according to a given model and not properly baptized, you were not capable of being a true Christian. Therefore, the Fernheim Mennonite Conference was not really a true Christian Church of Jesus Christ in the eyes of the other Mennonite churches in Fernheim since they were unable to provide an unambiguous certificate of the When and How of their conversion and they had also not been properly baptized. The fact that their walk in and of life was a credible testimony of their faith in Jesus Christ was simply not good enough. Another danger that Pietism presented is the matter of the internalization or spiritualization of faith. If I only believe in my heart that I am saved, then the practicalities of life no longer play an important role.

Resulting from the When and How of conversion, evangelizations gained ever more prominence. If you had not been saved under the sway of a prominent evangelist, your very conversion could be questioned. Being saved by the workings of the Holy Spirit without at least one minister being present now happened rarely. On the strength of mass evangelizations and definite forms of conversion, the workings of the Holy Spirit had, so to speak, become formalized. From now on annual evangelizations could be planned and subsequent baptisms planned in advance.

Although our father was in favor of evangelization, he still placed much faith in the freedom of the Holy Spirit. The Holy Spirit, based on the message of Jesus Christ, could direct people to a decision without a second party being present. Father did not want mass Christians but mature people who had wrestled their way to Jesus Christ in hard inner battles. Later, these knew whereof they spoke when they testified to their faith before they were baptized.

Further, father never insisted on a decision if he felt that the person in question was not ready for such a decision. He allowed his own children full freedom when it came to matter of decisions in faith. And one by one they all came.

The understanding of church and congregation, likewise, was a stumbling block for the Brethren. If the church consisted of properly converted and baptized members, then such surely constituted the virtuous bride before and in Jesus Christ, without spots or wrinkles. Father freely stated that he was still subject to battles and temptations in his own life. He therewith admitted that the Mennonite Conference church was no perfect church, but that it was one of members with mistakes and shortcomings on their way as followers of Jesus Christ. It would never happen to this church that it would not occasionally falter and do penance.

There were young people in the various villages who lived a spotless life. They had attended Sunday School and had participated in the various church programs for young people. They were to be seen at church practically every Sunday. If one were to have asked them, "Do you believe in God and in Jesus Christ?" the answer would have been a definite "Yes." However, for reasons only they knew, they procrastinated in their decision to get baptized and thus assume church membership. A young woman and church member was worried about her husband's spiritual welfare. When she approached father in the matter, he serenely replied,

"Give him time. He knows the path of salvation. If all church members led such an exemplary life as he does, the spiritual health of our church would improve and the reputation of our congregation would be enhanced. When his time comes to join the church, he will come. Then he will request to be baptized on his faith." That happened.

The purity of our church was a further concern. There were, in fact, ministers who smoked and smoking was regarded as a deadly sin. Was the church of Jesus Christ not meant to be without spots or wrinkles? Even Menno Simons taught so explicitly. In Menno's understanding of the church, as a virtuous bride of Jesus Christ, there is no room for sinners, even for good Christians who occasionally commit shortcomings.

In the many criticisms leveled at the Mennonite Conference by the Mennonite Brethren in Russia, these mainly quoted Menno Simons as their source and guide. Many members of the Conference were Mennonites in name only and even less Christian. Many of them obviously lived in sin. The fact that many Conference members were concerned Christians, who suffered mightily under the worldliness of their church was not accepted by the Brethren.

The document of separation by the Mennonite Brethren of 1860 was based mainly on direct quotations or paraphrasing from Menno's writings. The members of the Mennonite Brethren regarded themselves as the genuine Mennonites, the real bride of Jesus Christ without spot or wrinkles. And like Menno, who repeatedly demanded that the church of Jesus Christ shun the sinful world as did the Mennonite Brethren in Russia and the early decades in Paraguay, they demanded a strict divorce from the not properly converted and the not properly baptized, meaning the sinful Mennonite Fernheim Conference. A Mennonite Brethren woman who married a Conference Mennonite man, who had not become a Mennonite Brethren according to their demands and conditions, was excluded from their church. Things went so far that a teacher in a Fernheim Bible School stated to his students that he believed that all members of the Mennonite Brethren were converted, but that only the odd exception of the Mennonite Conference were truly converted.

Based on hard work and much patience, the obvious failings within the Mennonite Conference were overcome step by step. Due to the influence of the Mennonite Brethren Church and evangelistic workings from Europe and North America, real conversions became the subject of greater emphasis in the Mennonite Conference.

Due to developments occasioned by better educated Biblical scholars from within their own circles, there developed a more authentic understanding of the Biblical baptism which emphasizes not the How as much as the testimony of faith in Jesus Christ. Long before our father died, the Mennonite Brethren recognized the validity of baptism by sprinkling. Father, already in 1958, left it to the baptismal candidates as to which form of baptism they preferred. If they preferred to be immersed or dunked, he was prepared to do so.

For father, the form of conversion or baptism was not of first essence; the content came first. Have you really departed from the way of sin? Are you aware of the forgiveness of your sins? Do you believe in Jesus Christ as your Lord and Savior? Are you prepared to demonstrate publicly your faith by public baptism and to live your daily life according to this commitment? These were the decisive questions posed prior to baptism.

When father commenced his work as a minister at the Fernheim Mennonite Conference, the roads between the individual villages were constructed only by ax and spade. Means of transport were human feet, sometimes in shoes. If he, or any other minister for that matter, was to preach in a neighboring village, it meant walking. This meant a walk of one to two hours. Some of the more distant villages meant a walk of up to five hours. This meant that he had to start off already on Saturday. Later, when we had horses, he could ride. Sometimes oxen were hitched to the cart and the long, slow, arduous trip commenced. If this was the case, neighbors or family went along. This meant a leisurely trip, or the occasional diversionary walk alongside the vehicle with much conversation. This represented a great change for mother as well. She then finally had a day or two of rest. However, she did not altogether trust oxen after they had bolted one day and torn the wagon and harnesses to pieces.

Church work in the Mennonite Conference demanded much patience, wisdom and more prayer, in the beginning years. Church members came from various colonies in Russia. All had experienced the Russian Revolution. Particularly the men who had worked as orderlies in the Front during the First World War were not innocent, strange to the world, Mennonites any more. Most of them had experienced the anarchy with the wild gangs of Machnov. The burning, murders and rapes of these lawless bands had caused, or motivated, many Mennonite men to get involved in their own defensive internal Police Force known as the Selbstschutz. At that time, the dreadful famine ensued and then typhoid and other diseases befell them. Subsequently, the large independent farms were divided up and allotted to the landless. The hardworking farmers who had made Ukraine the breadbasket and granary of Europe were stamped as enemies of the people by the Communist government. The victims of these measures had become hard of heart, with some of them living immoral lives.

To constitute a pious church group out of such wayward pilgrims, required much wisdom, patience and love. In some cases, only hard measures were effective. If kind reprimands were ineffective, then they were excluded. In extreme cases, such sinners were banned. This meant that no one was allowed to interact with those so banned. They were isolated even in economic terms. Since there was no recourse for these Chaquenos, they admitted defeat, did penance, and asked for re-admission to church. Those not prepared to do so left the colony and lived in Asuncion or elsewhere to start a new life. Some of these families managed to do so, others dissipated and became degenerate.

During the flight, in the refugee camps, aboard ship, in the tent camps and even on their own yards families lived in close proximity to each other. There was hardly anything within families and even within married life that did not become public knowledge sooner or later. Since life in the enclosed wilderness of the Chaco offered no variety, and news of the greater world arrived very sparingly, these world-experienced colonists in the Chaco found life boring. Every out of the ordinary experience in a family, in the village or in the colony was repeated in detail, aka gossip. A neighbor with his wild oxen again plowing a crooked furrow on his field was a matter for lengthy conversational tidbits, and also ridicule. Every incident, even minute details, were of interest for the gossip mill. Gifted individuals, who told stories and invented tales were known and admired beyond many borders.

There was among us a good hunter who told breath bating stories about the hunt. When his wife one day corrected a tale, he responded in a perfectly serene tone, “So what if it did not really happen this way. People want stories, even if invented ones!”

The father of one of our family friends was a magnificent story teller. He was able to tell stories about the minor events of the day so interestingly, so accurately, and with so much humor that his audience never stopped laughing. When this family came visiting in the evening, we all sat around him in a circle and listened to his every word. Then our father, usually a serious man, laughed with all his heart.

However, it all became serious if you caught only segments of the story and had to compose the rest yourself. This was particularly the case when libeling cropped up. If someone lost a good reputation, it was next to impossible to redeem such sullied repute. Even if the innocence of the attacked party could be proven, a trace of the suspicion lingered.

One day a young man who had been accused of a serious transgression came to father. As vehemently as he insisted on his innocence, no one believed him. Father listened to him in due measure. Then father informed him that he would conduct his own research into the affair, requesting that the young fellow was to return in a week’s time. When he returned, father said, “We will both lose in this matter. I believe in your innocence and will continue to do so. However, this matter has become so widely discussed, that by now nobody wants to know the truth and even if I stick up for you, it is to no avail.”

It was sufficient for this young man to be believed by my father and was prepared to lay his good reputation on the scales of justice for him. He later stated that if Bishop Isaak believed him then it was quite enough for him. He was able to continue with his life despite all the charges and accusations. Years later after this young fellow had long left the colony, his innocence was finally proven.

Father struggled with libelous cases in the church and in the community all his life.

The strict self-appointed guardians of morals constantly tattled to father about their concerns. Imagine, the young men in the village dared to grow beards! Obviously this constituted a sin. Father countered by claiming that he liked a well cropped beard. If such were a sin, God would not have created man with beard proclivity. From then on, beards grew unclipped until the heat of nature made them shave off the facial fur. Or, women cropped their long hair, which, as an aside, was a clever thing to do, given the heat of the Chaco. Father had no misgivings about the matter and so they were spared church discipline.

At some other time some women and men of the church choir had been swimming in the Brazilian beaches, obviously in swim gear. Father himself loved salt water and the sea. However, for some of the church council this went too far. It was time to put down the foot on women who wore bathing suits, so it was thought. Father stated with great passivity that it would have been preferable for these concerned young men to have enjoyed the many beauties of God's creation. As it was, the moralizing Mennonite men and church leaders sat on the beaches and ogled at the Brazilian bathing nixes as they promenaded in their scant bikinis.

As to what manner of scenes their fancies imagined, only they knew; hardly such of stern virtue! Remember the words of Jesus when teaching that we become impure not through external impulses but by the lusting of our inner self. That was the end of that epistle.

There was little offered to the village youth by way of entertainment. The young people were allowed to get together only on Sunday evenings and play social games and sing old, weary and time-worn songs. These get-togethers were too much for the dear (moralizing at every turn) Mennonite Brethren and were forbidden in the villages in which they held sway. Blumenort belonged to the Mennonite Conference, and there the young people were allowed to kick up their heels to their hearts content. Such enjoyments attracted the youth of neighboring villages. Since many of these young people belonged to the Brethren Church, they exercised pressure on father to put an end to these social get-togethers.

When father gave in to their demands, a very mature refugee girl had an honest word with him. Did our father not realize that the young people of the Mennonite Brethren Church on Sunday nights disappeared in the bush and that merely holding hands was not on their agenda? If and when the young people gathered on the yards of their parents socially, such meetings were harmless and decent. Father admitted as much to the girl and social gatherings were not prohibited in Blumenort any longer.

When the mini-skirts were all the rage, father was disinclined to set limits on their usage. Rather, he was of the opinion that even fully clothed people were quite capable of provocative intent. Miniskirts were not necessarily the bearer of intent, the human heart was. This applied to the wearer of the skirt as well as to the beholder.

Home visits were part of father's work as a minister. These were mainly undertaken during the dry months of winter. If visiting a given village was due, he made his way there early in the morning. Father visited all neighbors, whether they belonged to Mennonite Brethren Church, the Evangelical Mennonite Brethren, or the Mennonite Conference. If he did not manage to complete the visit as planned, he stayed over till the next day. Father was a good listener and people soon came to confide in him, knowing that he honored confidentialities. Many people, including those from other churches, came to visit him as guardians of the soul.

When the economic situation improved, more and more young people attended university in Asuncion or even abroad. These students, who had lived a very protective life in the colonies, were now suddenly exposed to the secular culture of the wider world.

For many this transition was too radical and they executed summersaults of varying degrees. Most of them regained their bearings after a while and remembered the good which the Chaco offered. As mature people, they returned to the colonies to practice the trades they had acquired. To then make the transition to the very narrow-minded world of Mennonite church life in the Chaco was difficult for many of them. Many then came visiting father with all their many questions, knowing that Bishop Isaak would lend them an understanding ear and provide wise counsel. Also, specialized tradesmen from abroad found their way sooner or later to father where they could freely reveal their concerns since father listened to them patiently, and also explained to them all manner of things which appeared improbable to them.

When father once again visited a dear brother, this fellow told him about his dilemma. He was engaged in a quarrel with another brother in the village, knowing that he was right. Father listened patiently to the quandary without taking sides. Towards the conclusion of the visit, father prayed with him according to Matthew 18, for additional strength and love so that this brother, despite being innocent, would go to his neighbor and resolve the quarrel. Father had not yet left the yard when this brother already set out to resolve the issue. On the strength of God's love and power, this transpired.

Visiting the sick belonged to father's responsibility. At least once weekly he made his rounds in the hospital and visited all the sick. If the sick were at home, he visited them there. Often such visits meant taking longer trips if they resided in distant villages.

Part of the pastoral work was visiting smaller Mennonite groups who had left the Chaco. Some dozen families founded the village of Horqueta in East Paraguay. Others again found employment and living quarters in Asuncion. A larger group founded the Friesland colony. Young boys on the lookout for employment went to Bolivia to the large native ranches or factories in the cities. Since the climate in the Santa Cruz de la Sierra is much more pleasant than in the Chaco, a further group settled there in Bolivia. There in Cotoca, east of Santa Cruz, they founded the Tres Palmas Colony.

The ministers regularly visited all these groups in turn. Occasionally they officiated at weddings while there. Baptismal instructions were conducted and baptisms were celebrated. On Sundays, services were held and Bible Studies were conducted during the week. Invariably much spiritual counseling ensued. During the early years such trips took many weeks. Whenever father set out on these trips, mother was alone in the large household, on the yard and in the fields.

In his capacity as bishop, father's duties soon took him to neighboring colonies and into neighboring countries. When the Neuland Colony was founded, father presided at the baptisms and assisted in the election and ordination of the ministers. When this colony wanted to appoint him bishop, he declined. To do this by horse and buggy and the roads at the time, made this impossible. Then he was sent to Brazil to establish contact with the churches.

Father describes this long and interesting trip

to Brazil. Difficulties to that end started already in Asuncion, where he had to apply for a visa for Brazil. Since father was still stateless, a special visa had to be applied for at the government office. He spent his time in Asuncion visiting agricultural facilities in the proximity of Asuncion.

During this time and his location, a visit to Friesland to serve the congregation there was realized. The long absence from home became a worry. After seven weeks of waiting in vain, he was at the point of giving up and simply returning to his beloved Elisabeth and home. He knew how difficult the responsibility of house, home and family on his wife was. In his letters from Asuncion, he advises her to hire a hand to assist her.

Finally his visa was granted and he was permitted to assume his long trip to Krauel in the State of Santa Catarina in Brazil. Father boarded a plane from Asuncion to Curitiba, and this being his first flight, he made animated mention of it. When father experienced the Mennonite villages in the wild rain forests in the Brazilian mountains, he is not at all sorry that he did not decide to go to Brazil while still in a German refugee camp. Like on all his trips as itinerant minister, his days here were filled to a maximum with visits, discussions and sermons and spiritual counsel with ministers and deacons. Finally, this trip came to a successful conclusion.

In 1948 father was sent as a church representative of the Fernheim Colony to the Mennonite World Conference in Goshen and Newton, Kansas. This

Father and mother and their eleven children. Only the bigger boys wore shoes at the time. Money and leather were lacking for the younger set.

trip took many months since father availed himself of this opportunity to visit churches in Canada, as well as in the USA.

When Helmut later became the church minister in Greendale, many of the older church parishioners fondly remembered his father's visit in 1948. That visit transpired shortly after the catastrophic floods in the Fraser Valley. When father preached there in 1948, the church was submerged in two meters of water. There was no electricity in the sanctuary and so father conducted his service by the light of two candles burning on either side of the pulpit. Some of the church members there even remembered father and mother from Russia. Father had been their youth and choir leader in Memrik. For others, again, he had been their minister and spiritual adviser in Paraguay.

A proverb states that the parental blessings will build houses for their children. We children have experienced exactly the realization of this proverb repeatedly from our parents Jacob and Elisabeth Isaak. When word was out that Bishop Isaak was our father, many doors, previously closed, were opened to us.

In his report to the Mennonite World Conference on the Mennonite settlement in the Chaco father describes this highly controversial settlement project as a matter of faith. In order to establish an economically viable settlement in the inhospitable Chaco, most decisive prerequisites were lacking.

Grain farmers now became cotton farmers. Farmers, who had already started farming with tractors in Ukraine, were now meant to start breaking bush and land with axe and shovel and later with oxen. When they were finally able to provide for themselves, there was no market for their produce. From a moderate climate in Ukraine, they landed in an unpredictable climate with dreadfully hot and arid summers, to a green but mainly brown hell of the Chaco Boreal. Potable water was always a concern. Many died from malnutrition and from non-existent medical care.

But like Israel favoring the desert to Egyptian enslavement, these Mennonite pioneers chose the Chaco over Stalinist terror. Similar to what the Exodus meant for Israel, a matter of faith, so was the settlement of the Chaco a matter of faith. I believe today that this was a matter of God's guidance. Father placed that entire settlement project in the light of the Prophet Isaiah 55:8-9:

Grass huts in which the Lengua Indians housed when the Mennonites arrived.

> My thoughts are not your thoughts and My ways are not your ways, speaks the Lord; and as the heaven is higher than the earth, so are My thoughts higher than yours.

Father goes on: "While bowing to the Word of God and managing to become still, in the knowledge that we were being led by God, the Mennonite settlement in the Chaco of Paraguay...was a matter of faith for the settlers. And, possibly, this also held true from the very beginning for the MCC?"

For without the assistance of the MCC, the project would have failed. But their promise, "We will stand by you; you can count on us always," gave us, in our hours of greatest difficulty in our beginning years, the necessary support. Always.

After 18 years of pioneering, we managed to construct an economic existence, meaning that we had

Mennonite ministers with Bishop Martin C. Friesen from the Menno Colony fourth from left in the front row.

the basic necessities of life. But that was about all. The spinning and weaving operation planned by the MCC would not only stabilize our situation, but also greatly improve it. The price of cotton would rise accordingly and new employment opportunities would be given. But we will have to learn to live with the biggest problems, such as droughts, heat and locust plagues.

As compared to these negatives, there were the positive values like the freedom to live our faith as we chose, our conscientious status not to bear arms, our own schools with their own curriculum, the community of all children of God and the planning of our economy without state interference. These are all matters for which we prayed to God, and which God gave us in rich measure. These gifts and goods have endeared the Chaco to us and we would not exchange them for material goods.

The additional migrations of the Neuland settlers

will have a stabilizing influence on the colonies in the longer run. Initially, Neuland, a settlement consisting of mainly war torn widows and their fatherless children, represent a great difficulty in economic and spiritual terms.

The MCC should not neglect the care of these families, torn apart as they are, for a long time. It will take years until the many widows and orphans will become independent. Is the husband or wife still alive somewhere in Siberia? The children need a father and the single mothers need a man for their farmstead. The young men, who will arrive on the next transport, need women in order to found families and to start their own farming operations. Can the Mennonite World Conference help us in these matters? Can we marry these women and men if we do not know whether their partners are dead or still languishing in Siberian deportation?

With MCC assistance and with the experiences they have gathered, the new Colonies, Neuland and Volendam, will make more rapid progress than the Menno or Fernheim Colonies did. Father sees much promise for Volendam. The climate, the location and the soil are more favorable. The Frieslanders have proven this to be true based on their hard work, and even without any assistance from outside, or abroad.

A further duty for us in the Chaco is the Indian mission. We came to realize this shortly after our arrival in the Chaco. Already in our early years of settlement the churches together with the Frieslanders organized the mission society "Light for the Indians".

The Chaco War postponed the beginning of this work till 1935. Twelve years later the first seven Indians of the Lengua Tribe were baptized. A further three were baptized this year. We are totally mindful of the fact that we need to expand our mission work to all the people of the land. We have come to understand, in the interim, that God did not send us to the Chaco by coincidence. He had a great commission for us and this existed in us evangelizing the Indians and our Paraguayan neighbors.

Father invariably had the well-being of the entire community as his concern. Obviously his preeminent interest was the spiritual welfare of his own churches. However, he knew full well that the wider community as such was not sustainable without a healthy economic foundation.

To that end, he was constantly on the lookout for spiritual and economic potential. He always brought along new plants from his many travels with which he experimented in the Chaco. He experimented with coffee. When this plant sprouted and started to grow, expectations grew in direct proportion. Will we finally be able to drink real coffee again instead of substitutes? Or, he experimented with various fruits and berries. Top of the list were real potatoes. Yams and manioc simply did not stand the Mennonite test. But then the next drought and heat wave came along and these experiments quickly evaporated. Cattle breeding, and particularly milk cows, lay at his heart. As soon as the bush had been cleared and artificial, non-Chaco grasses could be grown, he bought better milk cows and was constantly bent on improving milk production. When the MCC developed an experimental station in the Chaco, he no longer had to conduct these experiments on his own.

When wheat production was successful in the Chaco, the hearts of grain farmers beat faster. You could again eat white bread, baked from your own wheat, milled in your own mill. Our father eagerly grew winter wheat. In the long run, however, it was not productive and had to be discontinued. In all of this, father never forgot that his chief responsibility was the care of spiritual life of the colony. God had specially called him to do so and this task was paramount.

Also, the connection to other colonies and churches was close to his heart. This led to a close relationship with Bishop Martin C. Friesen of the Menno Colony. Father describes the impression this great man made on him:

> Bishop Friesen, the longtime leader of the Mennonite Conference of the Menno Colony, was a man of sound, biblically founded faith. He was a man of tough will and firm character. He served the Lord faithfully and with great dedication in the church entrusted to him. His accessibility, his knowledge of the Word, and his circumspect reading as well as his humble piety as revealed in our conversations, and in common prayer, impressed me and commanded respect. His steadfast aim, and his stamina impressed me and his co-workers; his promoting the spiritual life in our colonies remain most

memorable. Now that he has had to retire for reasons of health he may well reflect on a life of successful work with a grateful heart.

It was father who first called the ministers of the Menno Churches to joint conferences to Fernheim. The Mennonite Brethren Church initially participated but then organized their own conference.

Father also established contact to the Danzig Mennonites and their ministers. They had fled from Prussia, to West Germany, or to Denmark during the Second World War. In the late forties they migrated to Uruguay. Here they founded the El Ombu and Gartental Colonies, then, later, the second generation started the Delta Colony.

In 1952 the General Conference requested father to visit the churches in Uruguay and to advise them on how to organize their churches. Together with Peter Wiens, he set out to do so. In a space of six weeks they managed to visit every colony and also the widely dispersed Mennonite settlements in the countryside, as well as in Montevideo. The Uruguayan churches were most thankful for this visit.

Finally, contacts were established to the South American Mennonite churches and later to the Brazilian Mennonites as well. However, it quickly became clear that they had brought along experienced and competent bishops from Prussia and that they had organized their churches in thorough Prussian style. Based on this visit a lively correspondence ensued between father and the bishop of the Danzig Mennonite Church in Uruguay.

Before long, they also attended the meetings of the Mennonite Conference of Paraguay and then the meetings of the Mennonite Conference of South America.

Even though some of the brothers in our church had reservations regarding the Danzig Mennonites because they publically drank wine and beer and danced at their weddings, a happy fellowship developed. It was particularly the honesty and humour of Bishop Regier who dispersed whatever prejudices that might have existed. It was also the deep piety of Bishop Dau and Dűck who won over people with reservations towards the Danzig Mennonites.

After father's first visit there, a brisk cooperation with the Brazilian Mennonites came to be. Mutual visits increased when this group left Krauel and resettled close to Curitiba.

Out of these initial visits regular and common endeavors were realized. First the Conference of Paraguayan Mennonite Churches was launched. This was followed by the founding of the Conference of the Mennonite Churches of South America. When in 1956 the Mennonite Seminar in Montevideo, Uruguay was opened, the Conference of Mennonite Churches of South America was involved from the start.

To the extent he could, father promoted youth work, first in his own church and then beyond the borders in cooperation with the neighboring churches in all of Paraguay. Later, holiday retreats and work camps were held in conjunction with the young people from all of Paraguay, Brazil and Uruguay.

In his talk regarding the task of the shepherds of the church, father refers to the dangers of political involvements and ideologies. As removed and isolated as the Mennonite Colonies in the Paraguayan Chaco were, they were not spared the great political upheavals of the twentieth century. Germany's National Socialism came calling among the Mennonites and caused one of the most severe crises among the Fernheim circles. Suddenly all settlers were supposed to be German and become German citizens as quickly as possible. Ten years prior Mennonites in Russia claimed to be Dutch for political reasons. Now these very same people based on political, or, more accurately, purely pragmatic reasons, were to become Germans.

But just how important or unimportant was the citizenship of a given politically independent state for Mennonites in fact and in reality? If one as a child of God is a citizen of His kingdom, is such not sufficient? Are we as Christians not above all pilgrims on and of this earth? Are we not first and foremost representatives in realizing God's Lordship here and today in this world, and only then involved in the politically structured involvements of the nations of this world? Had Menno Simons and the Anabaptists not thoroughly repealed the teachings of Luther and his Two-Kingdom Teaching aka dual citizenship of this world? As born-again children of God, we are first and foremost citizens of God's Lordship. We are to participate or get involved in the nations of this world only to the extent that it is necessary to realize an existence.

While the Swiss Brethren demanded a radical separation from the powers of this world, Menno left open the door for the possibility of a Christian society with a Christian government. In such a Christian state, the Word of God as interpreted by the teachers of the church was to be the ultimate authority. Already in Russia, but even more so in the Chaco, where the Mennonite Colonies operated, in practical terms, as a state within a state, Menno's vision could develop like never before.

When in 1930, Herald Bender at the Mennonite World Conference in Danzig, reported on the dire condition of the Mennonites in Russia, alternatives to avoiding catastrophes were deliberated. At that time Bender suggested that all Mennonite refugees be settled in the Chaco of Paraguay. There a Mennonite state could indeed be realized. Since the Chaco was practically uninhabited and Paraguay was perfectly willing to accept proven pioneers, the problem of stateless Russian Mennonites could be solved and resolved with immediacy and dispatch.

When Anabaptism started in Zurich in 1525 the right of citizenry in individual countries, the *Corpus Christianum* depended on the right Christian baptism in the Roman-Catholic church. Anyone not properly baptized by a priest of the Roman-Catholic church, and thereupon receiving a Christian name was stateless, without rights, and was regarded as a heathen or a Turk. For such there was no room in a Christian Europe, the *Corpus Christianum,* the body of Christ, and hence no possibility of life or living. Since the prevailing form of baptism and that of their children was not regarded as legitimate, Mennonites lost all rights of citizenship in their respective home lands. They lost not only all personal effects, but also every right to exist in Roman-Catholic Europe. When they at the time introduced baptism based on the personal testimony of faith, they were branded as the vilest heretics and most dangerous enemies of Christian Europe, who were to be exterminated on penalty of death, on the fire, by sword or by drowning.

These stateless Anabaptists, deprived of all rights, were the ones who fled to Prussia from the various European countries in the 1530's. Here they were tolerated by the Polish nobility, because they made the flooded areas of the Vistula Valley inhabitable due to their advanced technology in draining water. They had lost their citizenship in their home countries. However, they did not become Polish citizens.

When these various groups became more and more integrated into one body with their Low German language as a unifying factor, they developed a new and unique consciousness. They were not really Germans, Dutch, Swiss or Austrians. Granted, that the Dutch Anabaptists for generations to come retained the division in their faith between the Friesians and the Flemings, but in time they were known as what they were: Mennonites. Anyone not baptized on the testimony of personal faith did not belong to the exclusive Mennonite community. And just as previously in the *Corpus Christianum,* the proper baptism, meaning adult baptism determined membership of the Mennonite community, or, as of now, the *Mennonite Corpus Christianum*. When, in Russia at that time, and upon the will of the Russian government, enclosed Mennonite settlements were established, it was possible here and now, and exactly as on the *Corpus Christianum,* to acquire land, marry and attain citizenry only if one was properly baptized, meaning the *Mennonite* way. It is interesting to note, albeit not surprising, that in Russia the reference to Mennonites as a *Mennonite people* came to be. This *Mennonite people* now stipulates and formulates more and more the identity of its members. Since the colonies were in large measure autonomous, it was sufficient for most, that they were able to claim: We are Mennonites because we have been properly baptized. The proper form of conversion and baptism, in addition, was influenced by Pietism and Baptists.

When National Socialism was introduced to the Chaco by some hot heads in the 1930's, who had studied in Germany and the so-called People's Movement cropped up, it initially encountered consternation. We are, after all, the Mennonite people and in Paraguay we are a Mennonite State within the state. We never were Poles, Germans or Russians. And now that we live in Paraguay we are probably Paraguayans, if at all.

Our membership in the new People of God's Family is much more important to us than Paraguayan or German citizenship. But then when there was talk of re-migrating to Ukraine under German leadership many ears perked up. And certainly this was thoroughly understandable since the economic conditions in the Chaco at the end of the 1930's were still most difficult, if not indeed hopeless. Who would not have liked to return to their formerly beautiful farms in southern Russia and thrive to the heart's desire? If Communism could be vanquished and Ukraine incorporated into the German Empire, who would then not want to become a German? But when it became clear that conscientious objectors were not being tolerated in the German Reich, much interest waned.

These misgivings were countered by the leaders of the Nazis *People's Movement* in that they divorced the faith, induced as it was by Pietism and Lutheranism, from the political aims and structures of the Third Reich. No one would question the validity of their conversion or baptism. These leaders proclaimed moving testimony of their faith before their Brethren and church members. According to their convictions, Hitler was a sincere and serious Christian. The fact that he had to attack the enemies of the Reich with radical measures was simply necessary politics and had nothing to do with his personal faith in Jesus Christ. Based on purely pragmatic reasons many of the Fernheim Mennonites now chose to opt for the Two-Kingdom-Teachings of Luther, which they as Anabaptist Mennonites had formerly radically rejected.

The *Mennonite People* initially countered this new movement by resorting to their privileges. It was particularly the *privileged* c.o. status in Paraguay which they most decidedly did not want to lose. But then the prospect of tilling their land in Ukraine as *noble farmers* with rifle in hand gave pause to many. Father knew from his own experience how matters stood with the Mennonite People and their so-called c.o status. He knew all too well of the Self-Defense of the Mennonites in Russia. When in Communist Russia he had to appear before a judge and defend himself in his c.o. status, the judge asked him, "If you so radically reject every form of force, what would you do if wild bandits broke into your home to rape your wife and murder your children?" Father answered this question truthfully, "I do not know what I would do in such a case." Then the judge smiled, praised him for an honest answer and let him go home.

Father and mother were not, and never became Germans. If at all, they spoke of their Russian home but never of a German home. When they were offered German passports and therewith German citizenship, they declined the offer. They remained state-less during their first decades in Paraguay.

Father and mother did not get involved in the *Mennonite People's Movement*. When the National Socialists exerted their influence in the Fernheim high school, father took his boys out of the school. If, however, the People's Youth League invited him to speak, he did so. He used such opportunity to preach about a different Kingdom. He could then tell the young people about Jesus Christ, the Lord of Heaven and of earth. This Kingdom, which is already existent among us, has not been fashioned by the human hand. It is not vanquished by the weaponry of warring armies or defended by same. The weapons to that end are the gospel of Jesus Christ, divine justice, His truth and peace, which can overcome war. These weapons do not inflict death but fashion a full and eternal life.

As a child of God, father knew himself to be a citizen of that Kingdom. He served the Lords of the Kingdom with unconditional obedience. This Kingdom was eternal. In this life, father had already experienced the fall of two empires. He knew enough about the history of people to know that human empires come and go and disintegrate. The Third Reich, like all kingdoms before, would not be eternal. Just how absolute Hitler's dictatorship was and how inhumanly the Third Reich treated Jews and other minorities the Fernheimers knew only after it was all over. Father reportedly stated already in 1942 that the German war was over when he first heard of the fate of the Jews in the Third Reich.

In the meanwhile the quarrels pertaining to National Socialism in the Chaco became ever more vehement. As it has always been among Mennonites, various groups came into being within the *Mennonite People's Movement,* which waged enmity against each other. When this quarrel erupted into force on March 11, 1944 a group of young men from Blumenort intended to drive to Filadelfia. When father heard about this, he positioned himself in the middle of the street and said, "You are not going to Fildelfia today." That was all. They did not travel to Filadelfia. When father tried to do the same with another group in a neighboring village, they paid him no heed and left, much to their later chagrin.

When the National Socialist movement disintegrated in Fernheim, accusations mounted. In a letter father wrote to a friend in Canada, father stated, "We have all sinned." Although he and his family did not get personally involved, he, nevertheless, acted in solidarity with all Fernheimers. He went beyond that. Much injustice had been committed and many wounds had been inflicted. Reconciliations were called for. Endless discussions were held. In the final analysis, things were so bad that the very future of Fernheim was at stake, since a divided community in the Chaco could not survive. Finally, conciliations were celebrated, but not all participated to that end. Father also conducted a lively correspondence with some of the banned leaders of the *Mennonite People's Movement* and visited them in person when he was able to.

In 1937 Bishop Abram Harder was elected leader of the Mennonite Conference of Fernheim. Due to the departure and re-settlement of the Frieslanders, the membership of the conference had dropped sharply. However, the Conference had organized a powerful church council with nine ministers, four deacons, a bookkeeper and a secretary. Together with this staff, Bishop Harder set out to work. When this new church council met once a month, for an all-day meeting, further education for its members was on the agenda. This was to pay off in the long run.

When Bishop Harder gave up his office in 1948, Jacob Isaak was elected church leader. However, he refused to be ordained as bishop for now. Leading the church meant more work and responsibility for him and even more for mother. Since father now was en route on a daily basis, leading the household now fell on her shoulders.

It would have been wiser at the time for him to have moved to Filadelfia, where most of the meetings and programs were held. However, such was impossible for various reasons, foremost of which was that there were no farms available there. Since father was not paid for his work in church, even though some of his expenses were covered by the General Conference, our family was entirely responsible for meeting all expenses and costs.

To enable him to execute his voluntary services, father needed a team of horses. A team of horses and a buggy, plus a bag of horse fodder were mandatory five days a week as of now. The providing of such was done at the expense of the farm. Without the farm income, father was unable to do his work.

His wife Elisabeth and his many children produced the necessary income to support the family and to keep father's professional buggy wheels spinning. So father had to undertake daily trips to Filadelfia. It must be stated, that as dire as circumstances were, neighbors and other people helped out as best they could. Frequently a bag of kefir was loaded on the buggy by anonymous hands. In all honesty, father did not want payment for his voluntary work. His service and that of his family were rendered freely and without expectation of pay. Today we children, upon reflection, can and must admit, that all the work done, hurt or harmed no one of us. We were not poorer or richer than anyone else in our church. Thanks to the leadership of our farm operations, by father and mother and the many children, we were on par with the living standards of our fellows, our neighbors.

The meetings of the church council until such time as the church was built, were invariably held in individual homes. Since such meetings lasted all day, the respective mother of the house had to look after the midday meal. At the Isaaks, the meal was generally a roast chicken or a broiler with rice, sweet potatoes and manioca. When the buggies came rolling on our yard, the young roosters sensed trouble and took off. Our farm dog knew what to do and without much fuss assisted the rooster to roast in short order.

Father was born to the soil and would have preferred to stay home. He knew full well that his family needed him at home. Did he really have time for such a huge family? Were his demands on Elisabeth and the children excessive? If he occasionally expressed lack of desire to attend yet another meeting abroad, mother encouraged him to do so since she knew how much he and his services were needed. She would manage the farm operations together with her children. This troubled him. Did he not work overtime in the vineyard of the Lord? The fact that God blessed his work was obvious. But should God then not look after the material needs of the family? Why did Elisabeth and his many children have to work themselves to the bone while he was preparing sermons, making visitations, heading discussions and being available for others without pay or recompense? Why did he constantly bother himself with the problems of others when his own family so desperately needed him at home?

Just how desperately his children needed him at home is demonstrated by the following incident. One of his sons, Helmut, got stuck in Grade III and had to repeat the grade in public school. The spelling of the German language was no fun and he failed it. When one day he was preparing for a test the next day, his father sat down with him. Father dictated a segment to him with son harvesting red ink. The boy was close to tears. Father suggested, "Let us try this again." Patiently he explained to his son some of the more difficult words and their proper spelling. Then he repeated the dictation and this time Helmut managed to write it without more than a few trivial mistakes. The boy never again got an unsatisfactory grade in spelling. It was enough that the father sat down with him just once in his life to help him with his school work.

Father knew full well what a priceless gift he had in his Elisabeth, for it was she who made his work in church possible. Together with their sons in the field and the daughters in the household, she took to her many duties every morning with happy courage. She was the perfect custodian of farm and field as she daily assigned work to her children and supervised their labor. During harvests, when it meant feeding an additional twelve workers, she managed that as well. She was on her feet from early morning to late at night. When the field work was done, she sat for long hours by the light of a dim lamp and tended to the laundry. This meant shirts, pants and clothes which were in need of repair, stitching, washing and ironing. The whirr of the sewing machine was part of the nightly children's music. Patched pants at the time were no cause for shame, as long as they were clean.

Father owned only three shirts. One of them he wore, one was in the laundry and one was drying on the wash line. In winters during drizzling weather, as was invariably the case for days on end, this shirt failed to dry whether inside or out. Mother knew how to handle the situation: She got up at four in the morning and stoked the oven with hard wood. After an hour she shoved the red hot coals into the iron and work on father's wet shirt could commence. When father arose at six in the morning, his shirt, freshly ironed and comfortably warm was ready for pastoral service.

Once when father again came home late at night, he wore only his coat. When mother asked him about his missing shirt, he explained that he had given it to a fellow minister who had none. This fellow needed it more than he did, since he had several.

This time mother broke out in tears.

Father was constantly on the road, be it hot or cold, dry or wet. He could depend on his horses. When he was on his way home, his horses found their way home on their own. He could fasten the reins and relax and nod off. On one such trip, he and his trusted team were surprised by a thunder deluge. Since father was fast asleep and the thunder grew more boisterous, the horses recognizing a farm in a neighboring village, simply turned in and found shelter in the barn. When father awoke, the thunderstorm was over and he could resume his journey home although it took him awhile to find his bearings.

It also happened that father was asleep when they came home. Then the horses simply stood still by the closed yard gate and waited for him to wake up. Usually their wait was not long since mother had heard the buggy approaching and opened the gate. If that did not happen, our yard dog barked until mother or father awakened and the long day finally came to an end.

Our interaction with our house and yard dog had some peculiarities. We children were his best friends and we came and went and he never barked at us. Only on Sunday evenings, when we big boys came home late, he would bark under father's bedroom window until he woke up. Then, with a "Welcome home!" from our father we were able to go to bed. The next morning father got up to rise and shine earlier than usual and then he came knocking at our bedroom, saying, "Well, boys, if you need so little sleep, you might as well get up and start working." We dared not protest his timely wisdoms.

Father was soon elected to serve on the various committees in church. These were followed by local and international conferences. The KfK (Commitee for Church Concerns) highly valued him as a member and as a leader. Father's heart's desire was close cooperation with the other churches. Although the Mennonite Conference was allowed to work closely with the KfK, its validity as a church

The Isaak yard with Hartmut, our dog Greif, Hans and Helmut.

was often questioned. On the other hand, the genuinely converted and properly baptized members of the pure church had much opportunity to compare themselves with the *unclean* church. In this they invariably scored high marks. Proper conversions and baptisms of the *Conference* remained for years on end one of the main mission fields of the Mennonite Brethren Church.

After father had led and guided the Conference for four years he was ready to assume the bishop position of the church. As to what led him to that position and how he felt about it is contained in condensed form in his inaugural address:

> Dear Congregation! I have read about a famous learned man who one day was called to look at the corpse of an executed criminal. After he had viewed the face of the dead person for a

lengthy period, he directed the following words to his assembled students. 'Thanks to God's mercy bestowed in me through Jesus Christ, I today stand before you as your professor. I could just as well lie before you as the corpse of this criminal before you. Reason being: this man, whose life ended so tragically, was my childhood friend. We grew up together. We went to school together. Now he lies here as an executed criminal, and I stand before you, the much lauded Professor Heim.'

I feel similarly today when reflecting on my life. Most of my siblings, and friends from my youth were murdered, banned to imprisonment in Siberia, or they are today without state or home. Among the few who were saved were I and my family. This is nothing but a special grace of God's direction.

If I now reflect on God's direction in my life, I have to confess: through God's grace I am what I am. Once, I, too, was a slave of sin. But now I am a free person through my faith in Jesus Christ and a happy child of God. And that is not enough. In His great mercy, God has called me to His service. He has made me worthy to be His co-worker in His church here on earth. This is nothing I have earned but purely due to His grace.

Upon reflecting on my early times of service in my life, many experiences come to mind, in which, mindful as I was of my imperfections I cried out to God. "Lord, what shall I preach? What is it that you want me to say? And God came to my assistance. I know what it means: His power became mighty in me, a weak person. I became particularly mindful of my dependence on God when the leadership of the church was entrusted to me. Also today and since you have entrusted me with more responsibility, I have to confess my weakness with the Apostle Paul, so that the power of Christ may grow mighty in me. Based on God's grace, I am what I am. I know full well that I will never be able to execute my position as bishop on my own strength. I will only be able to do so by the power of Jesus Christ and your support. Therefore, pray for me, my dear wife and for our family, so that we together walk and act under the guidance and leadership of the Holy Spirit.

There is one matter I would like to address. My being ordained as your bishop today, happened not in aspiration of a particular dignity, but in order to attain your and God's blessing for this difficult position. I often lacked the biblical confirmation as church leader for this particular service. It happened upon your request and I today thank you for your trust and your blessing for my work. May God help me to faithfully execute this commission.

Through God's grace I am what I am. I am God's servant and also yours. Our relationship to, and with each other will remain the same. Please do not address me by the bishop title but simply as brother, because in the Lord we are all Brethren and Sisters.

Paul in 1 Corinthians 3:5 writes, "Who is Paul? Who is Apollo? They are servants and that is all." Further, Jesus said, "He who intends to be the greatest among you, let him be your servant." This passage represents a very clear task for me, and my wife is of similar persuasion. I intend to be your every servant, everyone of you, my Brethren and Sisters, and that with all my heart. You may count on that both day and night. Our house will be open to you always.

I am not lord over your faith, but, rather as Paul states in II Corinthians 1:24, "helpers of your joy," and that is what I intend to be for all of you: helpers of your joy, the joy in the Lord. I would like more and more to learn to be a helper for you. I intend to speak to the weary, to bring courage to the despairing, and to lead the sinners to Jesus.

We intend to build our church on the corner stone which is Jesus Christ (1 Corinthians 11). We intend not to build it on human principles which will not stand the Judgment Day. Our aspirations are directed on eternal values so that real fruits of the spirit may grow among us. To that end, I also invite our youth.

We are today particularly pleased that we have managed for years now in accord and love, together with the Mennonite Brethren and the Evangelical Mennonite Brethren, to do missionary work among the Indians and this work will continue. Dear Brethren and Sisters let us continue to stand shoulder to shoulder in the Lord's work.

The Lord has been merciful to us and He is so even today. May He be with us in the future and lead us. Pray with me as Moses once did, "Have I found grace in your eyes, so let me know Thy way so that I may know you and find mercy in Thy sight. Amen!"

The Commission for Church Concerns, short form KfK (CCC), is the umbrella organization in which all Fernheim churches were represented and still are. All matters of common colony concerns, be they religious, cultural or commercial were discussed and resolved by this committee; it had the final authority to do so.

Without the confirmation of this committee, no teacher and no civil servant in colonial administration could be hired. Even the chief mayor was answerable to this committee whenever irregularities in administrative matters surfaced, or if anyone acted too independently. It was reported that even father as head of the CCC occasionally went to this office in order to confront a respective head mayor or tell him bluntly: "This is not the way we do business around here. As a Christian community, we do not engage in smuggled goods even if are able to buy and sell them much more cheaply. We will not become involved in the general corruption of this country, even if it is occasionally difficult to draw a clear line in such matters".

In such negotiations father always remained neutral and stuck to the facts. He invariably differentiated between the problem and the party involved. He made the question under discussion his own and resolved it from such perspective and it became easier to find a common solution. On such a basis the cooperative effort between the CCC and the administration was enhanced.

The building of the church was already decided on in 1932, but the church simply did not have the necessary means to commence construction. When father visited the churches in Canada and in the USA in 1948, he took out loans at various churches and conferences while there, and these enabled church construction in 1949. A year and a half later, on December 31, 1950, the church was consecrated. The final building debts were not repaid until 1965. This House of God proved to be a real blessing for the congregation and for the Fernheim community.

In 1958 Canadian friends gifted father a delivery van for his work. From now on, he could master long routes in short order which previously took him many hours by horse and buggy.

However, this hardly meant that he now had more time for his family since as of now the church made even more demands on his time. For our farm, a team of horses was more feasible.

Was the van cheaper? By no means, since the fuel costs, plus maintenance were vastly more expensive than maintaining a horse and buggy, plus a sack of horse fodder. This type of vehicle was built for the German Autobahn and not for the dust and dusty

The Mennonite Conference church in Fernheim. On the meadow in the foreground today stands the Old Folks Home "Evening Peace."

Father and his old delivery van in front of the new church.

roads of the Chaco. The fine particles of Chaco sand penetrated every detail of the motor, and pistons and rings had to be exchanged and replaced on a regular basis. This cost much money. Even though our farm had become more profitable, most of the extra money from the milk and chicken operations now went into the maintenance of the vehicle.

If the auto mechanic had not frequently done the repair work on the van for free and not charged for the parts, the Isaak farm would literally have gone bankrupt on this time-saving van. But without the van, father was no longer capable of performing his duties. Even later, when the family moved to Filadelfia in 1963, our parents lived mainly from the income of the youngest son, Hartmut. He had in mind to continue his studies but he had to give them up in order to support our parents. Most of his income was swallowed up by the pastoral limousine aka vw van. Even when Hartmut was in Germany, he literally sent home thousands of marks to keep father's van afloat. Father got rid of this vehicle only after he was no longer allowed to drive.

Upon reflection, it was Hans and Hilda, Elfriede, Irene and Hartmut who mostly supported our parents. It was on the strength of their selfless labors that enabled father to work on a pro bono basis for the church and the community all his life.

After the sale of the farm, our parents were finally able to open a savings account. For mother this was new. Other women spoke of depositing savings on their account after the annual harvest. Mother said, she never had any idea what this meant. And now

Hans and Hilda on the Isaak farm in Blumenort.

they too had a savings account after having lived more than thirty years from hand to mouth. Thanks to the high rate of interest realized at the time, our parents were even able to bequeath some money to their children.

In 1960 father was involved in a serious accident. While en route to Asuncion he drove into a hole some three meters wide and a meter deep which the construction company had cut through the road in order to build a bridge. Since the Ruta Transchaco had not yet been officially opened, there were no warning signs posted at the work site. Father's van ploughed full speed into the hole, hitting the back embankment. Father hit his head on the steering wheel and was unconscious. Son Jacob broke his leg, while Mrs. Epp, a passenger, was most seriously injured. A passing motorist phoned the ambulance which delivered the wounded parties to the Baptist Hospital in Asuncion.

When one of father's good friends in Asuncion heard of the accident, he raced to the Bautista Hospital. Here he found our father lying on a stretcher in the open sun, since the orderlies had concluded that father was beyond all help. Father was then quickly rolled into the operating room. Father's skull been cracked. In order to repair the fracture, the whole lower jaw was attached by wire to the broken upper jaw. To facilitate drinking and the intake of a liquid diet, two of father's teeth were pulled. Everything healed together in time even though father did not manage to speak for weeks on end.

His Volkswagen was pulled to Asuncion and repaired. Since father had been en route on church business, they assumed the repair costs.

Bishop Harder, who stemmed from the Mennonite Brethren in Russia had managed to acquire respect and stability for the Mennonite Conference Church. Furthermore, he had established a good team of leadership. The church again started growing. When father then assumed leadership, the church continued to grow. This growth continued without interruption until, in 1971, when father relinquished his leadership.

Although father recovered well from the accident, he never fully regained his former vim and vigor. After he gave up the church leadership, he participated in the life of the church but only to the extent that his strength permitted. When the old

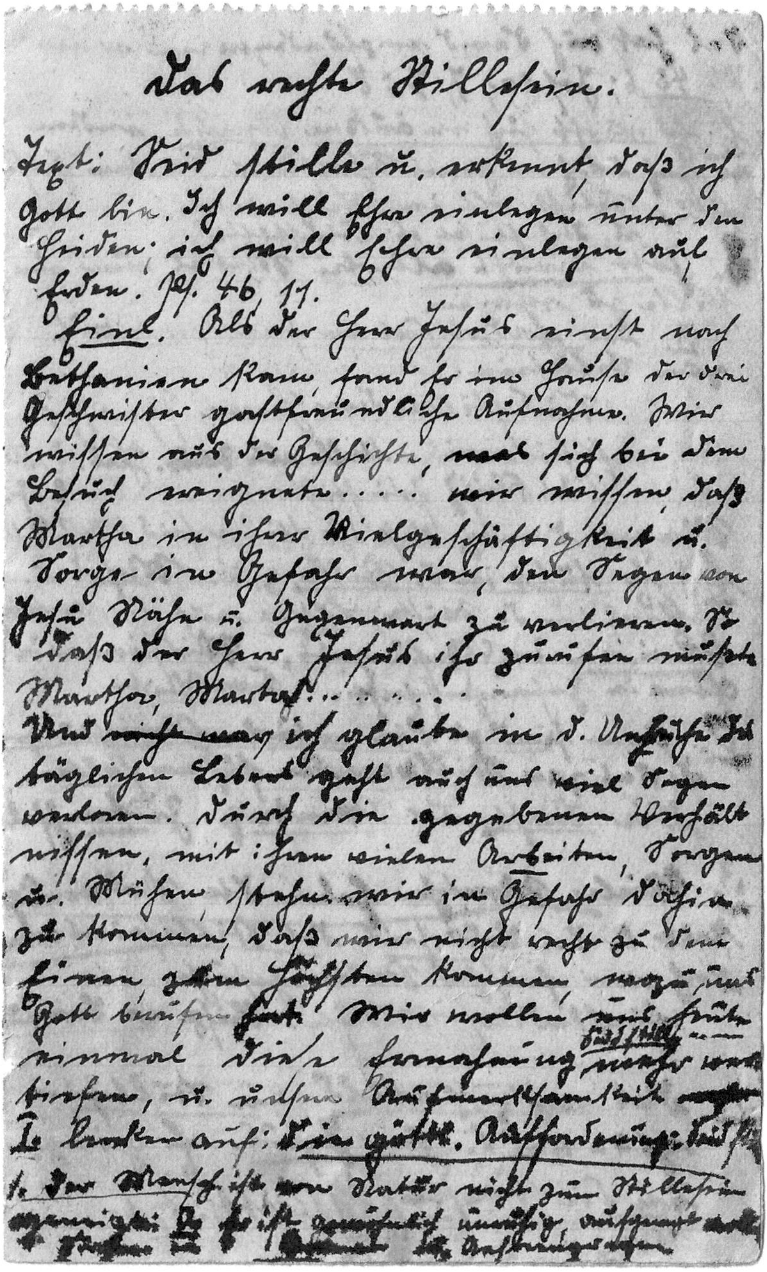
Das rechte Stillesein.

Text: Seid stille u. erkennt, daß ich Gott bin. Ich will Ehre einlegen unter den Heiden; ich will Ehre einlegen auf Erden. Ps. 46, 11.

Einl. Als der Herr Jesus einst nach Bethanien kam, fand er im Hause der drei Geschwister gastfreundliche Aufnahme. Wir wissen aus der Geschichte, was sich bei dem Besuch ereignete.... wir wissen, daß Martha in ihrer Vielgeschäftigkeit u. Sorge in Gefahr war, den Segen von Jesu Nähe u. Gegenwart zu verlieren, so daß der Herr Jesus ihr zurufen mußte Martha, Martha!......

Und nicht war ich glaube in d. Unruhe des täglichen Lebens geht auch uns viel Segen verloren. Durch die gegebenen Verhältnisse, mit ihren vielen Arbeiten, Sorgen u. Mühen stehen wir in Gefahr dahin zu kommen, daß wir nicht mehr zu dem Einen, dem Höchsten kommen, wozu uns Gott berufen hat. Wir wollen uns heute einmal diese Ermahnung [illegible] tiefer, u. [illegible] Aufmerksamkeit [illegible]

I lenken auf: Die göttl. Aufforderung: [illegible]

1. Der Mensch ist von Natur nicht zum Stillesein geneigt: [illegible]

A draft of a sermon written on a page of a note pad.

church became too small, it was replaced by a new one. Since father lived across the street, he followed the construction with great interest. He was impressed by the six-cornered structure and also he much favored the sturdy and massive walls. However, the 24 meter long flat roof did not meet with his approval. How were the walls meant to bear the weight of such a massive roof without supporting pillars? When father once again stood by shaking his head in disbelief, the constructor who greatly respected our father, had a mighty crane rolled into position. Then he attached the hook of the crane to a built-in hook embedded in the roof and lifted the entire roof a space off the retaining walls so that father could assure himself that the roof was strong enough to withstand the heaviest rains and storms. Father thanked him, now convinced. When he took his farewell, father still insisted that for the sake of safety one powerful weight bearing pillar should be put into place. However, even today, thirty years later that roof is just as stable as the day when it came to be.

Father wrote down some of his sermons fully and in detail. Most of his sermons though came by way of small notes with captive words. We have retained hundreds of these notes. It was a formidable task to de-cipher these notes for this author since they were written in the Gothic script. Secondly, in order to save paper and space, they were written in a tiny hand. Thirdly, the paper was of poor quality so that the individual letters are often no longer clearly discernible. In this I was dependent on my brother

Peter who can still read and write the Gothic script with fluent ease. With his help I can read father's sermons and incorporate them into the world of his theological deliberations.

Cornelius Isaak, 1928-1958.

CHAPTER IV
Cornelius

FATHER HAS ONLY WRITTEN in detail about one of his children, and that is Cornelius. When our parents settled on the estate in Auhagen in 1930, Cornelius was two years old. The Chaco with its heat and cold, rainy seasons and the great droughts, its luxurious growth of plants during wet periods, and its utter hopelessness when droughts hit, was the world in which he grew up. Cornelius was healthy, strong and highly gifted. Friends of his childhood describe him as daring, without being reckless. If he so chose, he did things that none of his peers dared to do. At the same time, he knew his limits and never sustained injury when he was up to something spectacular. He had a strong will but was not willful. If he decided to do something and was convinced that it was the right thing to do, he would muster all his strength to accomplish such resolve. At the same time he was a good friend and dependable. He never initiated a quarrel. If a quarrel broke out among us siblings or friends, Cornelius was invariably the mediator.

At the same time he was absolutely fearless. Once, when a giant anaconda came crawling out of the bush, Cornelius, with lightning speed, had a sharp spade to hand and attacked it. Since this variety of snake is very quick, it escaped.

An Indian Family in front of their little house.

The relationship of father and Cornelius was that of two friends, who, without wasting many words, got along excellently. There is one event which repeatedly comes to mind. Cornelius was already working as a missionary among the Chulupi (Nivacle) Indians in Filadelfia. We were at the time busily involved in renovating our old house. In addition to new roof paneling, a modern cistern was necessary. Cornelius arrived early on his bicycle from Filadelfia. When father greeted him, Cornelius immediately asked, "Where is the new cistern meant to be located?" Father showed him the site. Then they staked off a circle. After Cornelius had chosen the best available spade he remarked, that he would dig the necessary hole two meters in diameter and three meters deep by evening time. Father's response was a grin and "If you think so." Cornelius meant it. At ease, but decisively and quickly, he assumed his work. As the hole became deeper the work became more difficult since he had to shovel the earth out and constantly higher over the edge of the pit. Also, it became increasingly hotter in the pit. During the morning hours, we brought water by the pitcher to the digger, but later in the heat of day, he consumed water by the pail. From time to time father came around to watch without saying a word. By the evening, the pit was dug. After Cornelius took his leave, he mounted his bicycle and pedaled back to Filadelfia.

Father and Cornelius were not only friends, but they also worked together in church and on the mission field. When Cornelius came visiting on weekends with his family, he and father disappeared for hours on end in father's study.

We here include an abbreviated version of father's report of Cornelius's tragic death since this report has a lot to say about father and mother as well.

Our son Cornelius was born on June 13, 1928 in Karlowka, of the Memrik Settlement in Ukraine, as our third oldest son. He was physically and mentally sound and developed very well and was every bit as mature and intelligent as his two older brothers. As a boy and as a young man, he was invariably obedient and most diligent. He was always in a hurry as if he sensed that his time was limited. At the same time he was highly skillful and dexterous in all manual trades. He demonstrated these skills when he built his own house while working as a missionary among the Chulupi Indians. He drafted the building plan and built the whole house without a master builder; that building turned out to be a resounding structure.

While at school, Cornelius studied well and brought home good marks. He did well at Sunday School, which he enjoyed. He was a God-fearing boy. During his early youth, he experienced a genuine conversion under the guidance of A. E. Janzen. On October 1, 1944 he was baptized upon his confession of faith and accepted into the Mennonite Church. Shortly thereafter he was appointed as a Sunday School teacher, and at the age of twenty he was elected minister of our church.

Cornelius took his walk of faith seriously and led a pious life. He grew in mental and spiritual stature. When the call to become a missionary went out to him at age 21, he accepted it. He assumed this work together with Gerhard Hein among the Chulupi Indians close to Filadelfia. Jacob Franz, a missionary, taught him the Chulupi language. At the time he also studied for two years at the Bible School in Filadelfia.

In 1954 he found his life mate Mary Born. She gladly followed him to the mission field. She stood by him faithfully in oftentimes difficult work. Together they experienced the miracle of the grace of God when the Indians responded to the teaching of the gospel of Jesus Christ and were converted. Then the time came to instruct these new children of God in the teachings of Jesus Christ and to deepen their faith. Together they experienced much joy in their work.

They regarded their three healthy children as a gift from God, and accepted the news of their fourth impending child in the same spirit. With a cheerful heart and with God's help, and relying on His presence, they hoped to work for many years in the missionary field among the Indians. However, this blessed work came to an early end.

Unexpectedly, a call went out to Cornelius together with some other Brethren to establish contact with totally wild and very dangerous Ayoreos in the north of the Colonies. The time for a missionary involvement appeared to have come. After repeated deadly assaults on Mennonite Villages, and numerous belligerent confrontations with workers of the *Pure Oil Company*, who were looking for oil and gas in the northern Chaco, a friendly approach to these savages appeared not only possible, but also a given.

Since such attempts were coupled with mortal danger, Cornelius hesitated before giving his consent. Together with Mary, he sought God's will in prayer. After a week, they believed to have recognized God's will and they consented to this call. It was particularly Cornelius who believed that he had been called by God to this task. He pacified Mary's hesitation by quoting scripture, the Words of Christ. "He who loves father or mother, wife and child more than me is not worthy of me."

Our parents were not in favor of this undertaking. They made reference to his wife and children and his previously successful work among the Chulupi Indians. However, he was not to be held back. Then things happened as we feared they would. After a few days he was brought, mortally wounded, by airplane to the hospital in Fernheim.

The long line of people that appeared on September 12, 1958 at his earthly farewell appeared never ending. More than two thousand people,

Mennonites, Chulupies and Lengua were present to accompany their brother and teacher on his final earthly journey.

The mourners thronged in and outside the House of God. The modest coffin, containing the remains of the fallen warrior of the Lamb of God, was visible to only a few before the pulpit. All heard the moving words of a friend from his youth who delivered the eulogy according to 2 Samuel 1: "How the heroes have so fallen in battle. I am sorry for you, my brother Jonathan..."

He fell in battle for God's Lordship against the dark and evil forces of this world and that was exactly what this missionary, thirty years old, gave witness to with his life. Upon the command of his Lord, he sacrificed his life to bring the gospel of Jesus Christ to the savage Ayoreos. Equipped with the weapons: the coat of justice, the shield of faith, the helmet of salvation, the sword of the spirit, (Ephesians 6) he went into battle of the Lamb of God to proclaim the gospel to the Ayoreos.

The sadness of the Chulupies was stirring. They could not comprehend that their teacher had left them. Together they had read the Bible. Together they had followed Christ. Together they had been the church of Christ in the midst of this world. Cornelius and Mary with the children also belonged to their community. The color of their skin no longer separated them. They were altogether children of God and members of the body of Christ.

On that day of mourning, no one asked: Why did this young missionary, father, man and brother

The funeral for Cornelius Isaak, 1958.

Chulupies and Lenguas bidding farewell to Cornelius Isaak, their beloved brother, friend and teacher.

have to leave his life so early? Had there not been other, less dangerous attempts to approach the savages been given which would have spared his life?

Cornelius had supplied the answer to this question three weeks before in the same church, when, together with David Hein, he had been anointed for this special assignment. By quoting the Apostle Peter, he said at that time, 'We cannot help speaking about what we have seen and heard!' It is for this reason that he had to go, for the command of the risen Lord of heaven and of earth reads, according to Matthew 28:19, "Go forth and make disciples of all peoples!"

If hundreds of workers in their search for oil and gas risk their lives every day, how much more, then, should we as children of God be ready to risk our lives for the gospel of Jesus Christ? For many years the Mission Board had in vain sought to gain contact to the Ayoreos. Based on negative experiences of the past, with such going back to the Jesuit efforts to mission, these Indians avoided all contact with the white man. They became visible only for a few minutes, when they secretly attacked to murder and to kill and then to flee again into the density of the Chaco bush.

The northern Chaco had been their native home for hundreds of years and they defended it with every available means. When the Pure Oil Company simply rolled into their territory with their big and heavy machines, they were attacked by bow and arrow. It was particularly dangerous for small, isolated groups who were stationed in remote posts. During these sudden raids on them, deaths occurred.

When the three missionaries, the Lengua minister Seepe Lhama, David Hein and Cornelius Isaak took their first trip to the Ayoreos terrain, they traveled in their mission Jeep as far as Madrejón, the main camp of the oil company. They were allowed to pitch their tents here. The first reconnaissance expedition by the missionaries took them up to Cerro León. The Ayoreos had attacked this post most recently. They searched the bushes around their tents and by the landing strip but managed to find no trace of the savages. Further reconnaissance trips were also unsuccessful.

Finally, then, they followed an old bush path, much obstructed by bushes and undergrowth to the border fort of Ingavi. After some 54 kilometers, they arrived at a clearing near a lagoon. Even before the Jeep stopped, Seepe Lhama noticed traces of a fire.

When they then walked on a river bed, they found a smoldering tree trunk, scattered angling gear and three sticks stuck in the ground. Close by, another three sticks lay on the ground. The missionaries now shoved sticks of their own into the ground on which they fastened gifts. When they returned for the third time, they were overjoyed to find their gifts had been accepted. Upon further investigation, they discovered feather ornaments, fastened to a peeled red and brown painted stick. Next to the sticks was an empty wooden bowl with a few agave (plant) bulbs on the ground. Was this meant as a counter gift? The missionaries considered this to be the case. "Boghite duihoway!: We are your friends; we come in peace!" they called repeatedly into the bush. Then they expressed

Cornelius and Seepe Lhama at the site of the exchange of gifts with the Ayoreos.

The three red painted sticks and the empty bowl which the Ayoreos left for the missionaries.

gratitude to God for the answer of the savages.

However, Seepe Lhama later interpreted to his tribal partners the significance of their findings. The empty wooden bowl with the agave bulbs meant: We have nothing. There is nothing to be gotten here. The stick, painted red, implied blood. If you will come again, there will be bloodshed.

After they had left further gifts behind, they returned to Filadelfia to report on these most recent developments. Then Cornelius drove to Blumenort where his family stayed with our parents. It was a moving reunion. Many questions were asked and answered. The next day the three missionaries returned to Madrejón.

On the next trips to the lagoon, they again left gifts behind and discovered to their delight that these had not only been accepted, but that the Ayoreos in turn had left gifts for them as well. However, there was no sign of their physical presence.

Finally, on September 10th in 1958, the missionaries set out on their sixth expedition. Rain had fallen and the bush road was almost impassable. They got stuck in a mud hole en route. They managed to get the Jeep moving but only after much effort. The men again united in prayer. They gained confidence that God would be with them in this apparently futile undertaking.

When they came to a bend in the road, Seepe Lhama immediately caught sight of the Ayoreos. Having departed the bush, they were assembled in a large group, and looked expectantly at the missionaries' vehicle. The Indians at the front of the group were the only ones not armed. The missionaries jumped out of their Jeep and motioned for the Indians to come closer. Again they called "Boghite duihoway." The savages approached with quick, short steps. While doing so, they constantly grunted incomprehensible language among themselves. One of them grabbed the shirt which David Hein offered him. In return he offered him a bag made of cactus filaments. He took the shirt but held on to his bag. The others also accepted the missionaries' presents but held on to their feathered decorations. This caused alarm among the missionaries.

Then, suddenly, the Indians attacked. One of them threw his spear from a short distance directly into Cornelius's back. A second aimed an arrow at David Hein, but did not release the arrow. Other Indians tried to wrestle Seepe Lhama down and tie him up. Cornelius pulled the spear out of his back and, strangely, found a weapon in his hand. When Seepe Lhama managed to free himself, he pulled the hunting rifle out of the Jeep. When the savages observed this, they quickly retreated into the bush and deliberated as to how things would now progress. While David Hein stood in the middle of the road with his rifle, Cornelius managed to man the steering wheel of the Jeep in order to take off. He urged his men to hurry, knowing that he had been seriously injured. After a brief spell, David Hein had to do the driving since Cornelius was too weak to continue. Although his wound bled only a little, Cornelius slowly lost consciousness. Seepe Lhama supported him as well as he could, and David Hein attempted to avoid holes in the muddy road. They managed to ford the mud hole without too much difficulty on the return trip. When they reached the camp, pain relief was administered to Cornelius. Fortunately the (Oil Company) Cessna plane was available and Cornelius was flown to the hospital in Filadefia where they arrived at 11 AM.

The news that "Cornelius Isaak had been mortally wounded and delivered to the Filadelfia hospital" spread like the wind through the Chaco and then abroad. Mary and her children and both families gathered at the bed of the seriously wounded Cornelius. He had regained consciousness but was obviously getting weaker.

When the physician, Dr. Rakko arrived from a neighboring colony, he observed internal bleeding. Cornelius' brothers, who shared an identical blood type, donated blood. Finally the physician had to resort to surgery. The operation revealed that the spear, aimed for the heart, ricochet off a rib and then injured the spleen, pancreas and a kidney. When Dr. Rakko managed to suture all these up, and even managed to stop the internal bleeding, he was optimistic. He had every reason to believe that such a strong young man like Cornelius would recover soon, he noted in his report. But things turned out differently. Early the next morning, with a prayer on his lips for his family and particularly for the Ayoreos, Cornelius Isaak passed away. His blood did not coagulate; this was a sign that the spear was poisonous.

Devastated, the two other missionaries returned to Filadelfia for the funeral of their friend and brother.

News of his death reached them while they were peacefully playing and eating with some fifty Ayoreos outside the Oil Company's camp. At the funeral, David Hein reported in detail of their last trip with Cornelius Isaak and the tragic end. He also reported how the Ayoreos, upon his return there, had peacefully awaited him. The Ayoreos returned to the camp the next day and acted as if nothing had happened.

David Hein also reported that the Paraguayan government had declared open season on the Ayoreos. They had dispatched troops into the area with an order to shoot any Ayoreo they encountered. At the conclusion of his address, Hein said, "Who of you is prepared to return to the scene with me before the troops arrive? Who will fill the gap of Cornelius Isaak?" His call was not in vain. The next morning he returned with three young men to the Ayoreo area. He intended to prove to the Indians that their bloody deed had nothing to do with the love and friendship of the missionaries who had come to bring them the gospel of Jesus Christ.

The name of the young Ayoreo warrior, who had mortally wounded Cornelius, was Jonoine. He was a strong and ambitious young Indian whose aim it was to become an Indian chief like his father. Like all nations, which send their young men to war to defend their mother country, the Ayoreo men defend their native lands against the invasion of the white man. Jonoine is no murderer, but a warrior and a hero who merely did his duty and risked his own life while doing so.

After the tragic encounter with Cornelius, Jonoine

Mary and her children, after the reconciliation with Jonoine.

withdrew to the northern Chaco and beyond to the border of Bolivia. When his tribe finally gave up the war against the invasion of the white man, he finally came out of the bush. He became a Christian at the New Tribes Mission station. It was then that he was reconciled with Mary and her children as well as with the Isaak and Born families.

Helmut, number nine of the Isaak family, met Jonoine for the first time in May 2009 at the Mennonite Word Conference in Asuncion. While there, Helmut extended a hand of reconciliation to Jonoine. At that occasion and in front of a large audience, Helmut said:

> Jonoine, fifty years ago you were a strong young warrior of your people. You defended your homeland against the invasion of the white man and became a hero to your people. Fifty

years ago another young man, my brother Cornelius went to war for the peace of the Lamb of God. He also was courageous and strong. He also was prepared to lay down his life for his Lord and Savior.

Jonoine, you acted according to the values and customs of your people. My brother did what he had to do in accordance with the command of the Lord of heaven and earth. When the two of you met for the first time on the road to Ingavi in the Chaco, my brother lost his life. Jonoine, today we are no longer enemies. Today we are brothers in Christ Jesus. Today we together fight the war of the Lamb of God against sin and death.

Jonoine's answer to Helmut's words were:

When we still lived in the bush we had different habits and customs. I was a young warrior and intended to become a chief of my tribe. To that end I first had to kill an enemy. At that time we did not know that some white men were peaceful. We did not know about this difference. For this reason I killed the white missionary when we first met in the bush. I did not know about his good intentions. One of our old chiefs demanded an answer from me for my deed because I had endangered the peaceful relationship with the white man. Today I, too, am a Christian and ask myself time and again: Why did I kill the missionary? Today I am an

Reconciliation with Jonoine at the Mennonite World Conference in Asuncion, Paraguay in 2009.

The widow Mary with her four children, Corny, Rudolf, Rita and Siegfried.

> old man and dependent on the support of others. Can you support me in any way? Another matter on which I often reflect is: When Christ comes, I will be able to greet the missionary whom I killed as my brother.

Unfortunately, the leader of the worship service did not allow Jonoine to make this statement in front of the large congregation. It was sent to me later and was then published in various Mennonite publications.

The Chulupie wanted Mary and her children to continue to live in their community. They promised to look after her needs and those of her family. The Mission committee had other ideas. It built a roomy house for her and her family in Filadelfia and looked after her livelihood. However, it took many years for her and her family to come to terms with the death of her husband, the father to her children. Father and mother grieved the death of their son for the rest of their lives.

Father concluded his report as follows:

> For Mary things are becoming more difficult. She has been very courageous up to now. But the sad fact remains: Corny will never return and this sadness is increasingly setting into her consciousness. She is constantly becoming lonelier and this is threatening to overcome her. The older boys long more and more for their father to come home. Things will become even more difficult for Mary. Pray for her!

CHAPTER V
Father's Theology

FATHER NEVER WROTE out his theology systematically. The following is a summary of his many sermons and presentations.

Father's theology developed out of the rich and difficult experiences of his life. Particularly in his young years he constantly experienced how plan after plan failed. First he wanted to study, but the Communist Revolution destroyed this plan. Then, together with his friends, he drew up plans to migrate to the USA via Batum. Then he fell seriously ill of malaria and again his aspirations failed.

He became acquainted with Elisabeth Hildebrandt, his future wife, from the Memrik Colony. When they married, the Soviet government had temporarily adjusted its economic policies (NEP), which caused the Mennonite farmers to gain new hope. They hoped that things would improve in Russia, after all.

Father had already intended to migrate to Canada in 1925 when it was still possible to do so. To that end, they had sold their Chutor and would have been able to start anew in Canada. But at that time, his parents in law and a brother in law were not prepared to join father and mother. These family members persuaded our parents to stay, but father knew already then that he had passed up a glorious opportunity to leave a troubled country.

When in 1929 they abandoned everything in order to leave Russia via Moscow, they, the Isaak family, together with thousands of others, ran the extreme risk of being deported to a life-long ban to Siberia. However, this time, together with six thousand other fortunate ones, they were allowed to migrate to Germany.

When they arrived in Germany, the next disappointing news hit them. Canada and the USA had closed all borders to refugees since the unemployment rates due to the Great Depression were such that they were unable to accommodate new immigrants. The refugees were not able to remain in Germany either. When a possibility was given for them to remain in Germany, father had come to realize that Germany was not the promised land for him and his family. After he had also struck Brazil from the land of a new start, only the dreaded Chaco of Paraguay remained as their future home. This was the promised land God had chosen for His resistant servant and his family.

This, then, was their promised land in which he was to make good on his vow, "Lord, if you will deliver me and my family out of Communist Russia, I will serve you." When he made this vow, he had had Canada or the USA in mind, but certainly not the Chaco of Paraguay. However, God allows no bartering with Him.

When reflecting in his later years on God's wondrous ways and directions, father concluded with mounting clarity that all the shattered plans and disappointments of his young years were nothing but preparations for his service in the Chaco. Only the battles and experience in real life prepare us for the unconditional service of the Lord and no theological education or training in higher institutions of learning serve as an alternative for such practical ventures.

Now the significance of the inner voice at his conversion "All you have to do is believe" became clear to him. "Belief" means, foremost, accepting the forgiveness of sins through the cross of Jesus Christ. We have been set free of sin and guilt by grace. We no longer live under the forces of this world. God has done this for us in Jesus Christ.

The second meaning of "belief" which cannot be separated from the first meaning is the new life in the Lordship of God. Jesus calls us to his discipleship. We have been freed from the enslavement of sin and the forces of this world in order to fully live according to the example of our Lord and Savior Jesus Christ. This means that we are now called to live our full life in His Will. We are called not to rule, but to serve. Instead of judging, we are meant to forgive our neighbor his guilt, his debts. We are to share our goods with those who have none. We see the loneliness, hunger and thirst, the suffering and the enslavement of our neighbor and we help him selflessly like God has helped us through Jesus Christ.

We, as people and even as ministers or bishops, can save or convert no one. Conversion is the work of the Holy Spirit. This can transpire in the twinkling of an eye or it can take years. We can and shall cast the seed of the Word of God but only God can realize growth and development.

In this process, the When and How of conversion plays no role. The only deciding factor is that I listen to, and accept the call of Jesus to follow Him by knowing that Christ also died for my sins and that God has accepted me as His daughter or son.

Neither is the form of baptism decisive. It is important that I, as a born-again child of God publicly profess that I have become a child of God and that I therewith join the community of believers and that I accept the responsibility of God's Lordship.

This being born anew, or more accurately, this being born again from above changes all of life. In the first place, it changes our relationship to God, who in Jesus Christ becomes the father of the lost son for us. Our relationship to this earth on which we live changes altogether. We do not own it, we do not exploit it, we do not contaminate it. As God's creations we tend and nurture it and look after it in such manner that its fertility produces a surplus for all creatures to live and exist.

Our very relationship to ourselves changes fundamentally. I am a child of God and a citizen of His Kingdom. As followers of Jesus Christ we, too, are co-workers and co-heirs in his Kingdom. To be sons and daughters of God is a dignity which far outranks all titles and honors of the kingdom of this earth. This incredible dignity does not render us arrogant or desirous of power but is realized in humble service and in love to our neighbor.

Since I have been converted from above as a

born-again child of God, I know that I am created by God just as I am. Since God accepts me as His son or daughter just as I am, I have to accept myself just as I am. Only then can I overcome my weaknesses and shortcomings and properly develop my gifts.

The most difficult reality to put into practice is my new relationship to my neighbor. He and she have been likewise called to be a son or daughter of God. For them, likewise, God has prepared a fullness of life. He or she likewise stands before God and is solely responsible to Him. God has given them a dignity on par with mine. I am not allowed to be envious of their gifts, nor am I allowed to impede the developments of these gifts. Neither am I allowed to judge them with pious words or slander them or bear false witness against them. I am no longer envious of my neighbors nor am I covetous of whatever God has gifted them.

My highest task is to help my brethren and my sisters in the realization of their new life by being their helper as God intended it. For this reason, and to that end, I am to help them in bearing their burden. If my neighbor gets lost I am not to stand by and judge and measure and condemn. It is much more my duty to search the lost sheep and to restore it to its proper path. I cannot do so in my name but only in the name of our Lord and Healer, Jesus Christ.

As one who has been converted from above, we now live as sons and daughters in the Lordship of God. We are co-workers of Jesus Christ in the building of His Kingdom. This Kingdom towers above all the empires of this world. To be citizens of God's Kingdom, ranks higher than citizenship of any empire of the world.

From now on, we live, first and foremost, according to the Will of God and only then in accordance with the laws of the rulers of this world and only as long as they do not contradict God's commands.

In God's Kingdom, we as converted children of God are all equal. Color of skin, our education, our social status, our language and our culture are inconsequential.

In the kingdoms of this world we are Russians, Dutch, Germans, Canadians or Paraguayans etc. In the Kingdom of God we are all sinners, who have been forgiven, but lack the honor which we are meant to have before God (according to Paul).

As children of God, our identity is determined by the Lord of heaven and earth which is Jesus Christ and not by the powers of this earth.

The citizenship of God's Kingdom is not exclusive but inclusive. This means that all races, peoples and nations have been called to be His children. They need only believe and to be obedient in order to belong.

Although we are still citizens of the countries of this world, our unconditional loyalty belongs above all to the Lord of heaven which is Jesus Christ.

Father did not accept Luther's Two-Kingdom-Doctrine as it was implicitly propagated by the Peoples' Movement (NSDAP), any more than did the Anabaptists. To that end no pietistic holiness and internalization of faith made any difference.

As a community of converted children of God we are still, and constantly en route towards perfection. The pure congregation as the perfect, immaculate bride of Jesus Christ will come to be only in the new heaven and on the new earth.

Many spiritual gifts are given for service in the church and for our fellow man. Some of these will become evident only when they are needed or required. Father believed that he was tongue-tied like Moses. Or that he was unclean of lips like Isaiah. But all that was of no avail to him. God had called him, just as he was, for a special service and He shattered all other plans for his life until he humbly went there where the Lord needed him.

If we humbly enter the service of our Lord and Savior and go where He wants us to go, then all earth will again become God's creation and the promised land for us. This applies even to the disreputable Chaco of Paraguay.

By preaching the Gospel of Jesus Christ we help in the distribution and the building of God's Kingdom. The command of the risen Lord of heaven and earth, "Go and make disciples of all people" applies to every citizen of God's Kingdom. In so doing the witness of our daily life speaks a more forceful language than preached words ever can. Words can have many meanings and depending on circumstances, can be interpreted in various ways. However, selfless service to our neighbors in the name of Jesus Christ cannot be misunderstood. For this reason all children of God, on the way of discipleship, are evangelists in the best sense of the word.

Evangelizing and conversions were invariably important events for father in the life of the church. However, conversions were only the introduction into a new life in God's Kingdom. With it the new life on the way to following Jesus Christ was only the beginning.

Upon conversion we reject the norms and the values of this world and accept the values and the norms of God's Lordship.

We reject the old me dissipated by sin, and accept the new me, to which we are born again to, in accordance with the image of God as revealed to us in Jesus Christ.

The newly born-again individual, born-again from above, continues to live in the kingdoms of this world with all its temptations. In order for us to overcome them we are dependent on the weapons of God's Lordship as we find them listed in Ephesians 6:10-16. And the more we practice use of these weapons of the Lamb of God, the more effective we become in our battle against the enslavement by sin and death.

The gifts of the Holy Spirit are available to all who stand in the service of God's Lordship and therewith in our service to our neighbor. For this reason, neither lofty titles, nor the great institutions of Christian churches will play any part or role at Judgment Day. The decisive question is: Have you given the hungry to eat, given water to the poor, taken in the stranger, clothed the naked, visited the sick and gone to the prisons to attend to the inmates (Matthew 25:31-40)?

CHAPTER VI
Correspondence and School

FATHER WROTE MANY letters in his life. He corresponded with his brother Heinrich and his brother in law Cornelius in Russia. When his children then attended university abroad or migrated to Brazil, Germany or Canada, he regularly exchanged letters with them. He also wrote many letters on behalf of the church, the Conference and the community.

Good schools and higher education, in addition to his work as shepherd of his church were of great importance for father. Since spiritual development of young people must be attended by educational growth, father encouraged both. When the Middle School in Fernheim had to be shut down due to a shortage of teachers, he wrote constantly to sources further north, pleading for competent teachers to be sent to the Chaco. Father was also much interested in adequate professional training in the trades. He invariably sought to find the necessary funds to finance bright young students to attend universities in Paraguay or abroad.

In the beginning years, father wrote with pen and ink. Then he was gifted a typewriter. Now he could also make copies of his writings. He used the ribbon until it was punctured with holes. He replaced the carbon copies only when they went “colorless”. He had no alternative, but to pound all the harder on the keys for the paper to record his message.

Father also conducted a wide-ranging correspondence with Dr. Rudolf Dyck. The contents of this exchange is here recorded in his own words as his letters reveal:

> Bishop Jacob Isaak played a decisive role in my professional life, starting in the Middle School right up to my university studies. His involvement was never apparent, except that his goodwill, intentions and wisdom were my direction and my guide.
>
> I do not know when the friendly relationship between my parents and the Isaaks commenced. However, it may well be that many of his relationships were seamless since his manner was effortless and compelling.
>
> I was particularly impressed in my early youth by a church celebration at which the minister, Jacob Isaak, was ordained bishop; this celebration was conducted in accordance with the Russian-Mennonite tradition and a visiting bishop from our Conference, Bishop Gerhard G. Neufeld, from Canada was invited to attend.
>
> It was at this time while attending the Middle School during a personal discussion with Bishop Isaak in which I made a decision for Christ. I was baptized that very year by him in December 1947, together with a group of mostly young people from Neuland who had recently arrived.

As a recent member of the church I was impressed with the gentle and persuasive approach he dealt with all questions posed to him. For example his contemplative demeanor stood the first baptism of recently converted Indians in good stead. These had come to their faith by a missionary program launched by all three churches involved. Here baptism by immersion was practiced. This led to questions in our congregation. His gentle response was simply that the form of baptism was secondary to the acceptance of faith and was accepted as such.

It was my personal professional aspiration to study medicine. However, my ambitions to that end went unfulfilled.

Together with a former teacher, who had come from Canada, and was active in our Conference, we cast about for possibilities for me to realize my professional dream. Argentina was chosen as the land of study and he helped me in facilitating my studies there. This assistance in practical terms was unique. The possibility of carrying out this plan of assistance played a secondary role for me at the time.

Obviously my future plans had become known to other parties at the time but without my knowledge. And it was again Bishop Jacob Isaak who facilitated everything and realized concrete steps to make my studies a reality. A few weeks before my departure, Bishop J. J. Thiessen from Canada, was visiting our colony. He was responsible for various assistance projects abroad. He was informed by our bishop about my professional ambitions. A short discussion between us was all it took. He simply stated after 15 minutes, "Just leave and try to gain entrance and if you manage it, we will help you." What he meant was that I was to resolve the technicalities of admission to medical studies.

The necessary information for the next steps to be taken had been gathered. This procedure was complicated by the simple fact that I did not have the legally stipulated credentials of my previous educational records. To that end, I had to start all over again. My benefactors in Canada and Bishop Isaak were kept informed of my progress. At times I made oral contact with them as to the progress of my preparations and arrangements.

As I approached my professional goal, Bishop Isaak demonstrated his help by offering unconditional and absolute faith in me. Soon my scholarship from Canada was provided without any obligations on my part. All they requested that I spend two years as a professional physician in Paraguay for every year they had provided support. The probability of investing a quarter of a century appeared an eternity for me at the time.

During my next visit in the Chaco in the following year, I informed Bishop Isaak about my problem. He probably read my demeanor accurately when stating, "Just leave the matter be, I will resolve it."

I do not know what he communicated to the Canadian authorities regarding this matter. All I know is that all the troublesome demands and conditions by the Canadian Mennonites were summarily dropped. And if not, the benefactors gave me seven years in which I could re-pay scholarship monies received. This arrangement appeared generous enough for me to accept. For my young wife and me our decision to return to Paraguay was clear.

After a year internship in Buenos Aires my wife, who is also a doctor, and I went to the promised assignment. From now on, the respective site of medical employment had two doctors instead of one. In the course of many years, Bishop Isaak was a widely sought out counselor and not only in spiritual matters for the colony but also beyond. His promised word and his sermons never contradicted the realities of life in the rough. For many others, but for me in particular, his work was a blessing.

Dr. Rudolf Dyck was mother's and father's medical doctor when they resided in the Old Folk's Home in Filadelfia. He cared for them in exemplary fashion. There was only one point in which the two, my father and Dr. Dyck, were of varying opinions. According to his medical opinion, our father lived much longer than he was medically entitled to. However, father waited for his son Hartmut and his family to return from Germany. When he finally did return, father died within days. On the other hand, we owe

Dr. Dyck grateful recognition for having kept our father alive for as long as it took for his final wish to get fulfilled. In the name of the Isaak family we here want to express our heartfelt thanks to Dr. Dyck for his every deed.

In 1978 one Jasch Klassen from Canada wrote the following lines to our father:

> I would like to thank you from my heart for everything you did for me in my youthful years. A teacher who taught the clear Word of God; a counselor whom we could approach in confidence; a custodian of the soul who cared about our spiritual life and not least of all a shepherd, who watched over all his church. I thank God from my heart that I personally experienced so much love and tending from you.

A vigorous correspondence developed between mother's sibling, Cornelius and Maria Hildebrandt in the 1960's. They reported about their family, relatives, the weather and commercial matters. And so mother's brother Cornelius informed her in 1972 that their father had died in Karlowka in 1941. He was simply tired of life and he died peacefully. Our mother's mother died in 1944 when typhoid ravaged the villages. There were so many deaths that the corpses could not be buried until spring. When his mother died, Cornelius was working in a coal mine and he was not able to arrive before spring at which time he buried her.

The entire Hildebrandt family managed to

migrate to Germany in the nineteen nineties. Mother's brother was the last one to leave Russia. We, as the family, had planned a huge celebration for mother's ninetieth birthday, at which all family members planned to be present. Her brother Cornelius, whom mother last saw in 1929 also planned to be present; to that end he planned to fly in from Germany. Mother and her brother were overjoyed. This celebration was also to be special for the Isaak family. For the first time in their lives, they would meet a real uncle since father and mother's siblings had all stayed behind in Russia. Unfortunately things turned out differently than planned. A few days before his departure, Uncle Cornelius died in Germany. The incredibly hard work in the forced labor camps and famine had so much diminished his strength that he could not come to terms with the great joy at seeing his sister again. This was a hard blow for all concerned. However, a few days earlier mother and her brother Cornelius had spoken at length by phone. In spite of the sadness of the uncle's death, mother's ninetieth birthday was special. Mother beamed like in former days since she had all her living children with their marital partners as well as a huge number of grandchildren and great grandchildren present.

Father also maintained a lively correspondence with his brother Heinrich in the 1960's. Brother Heinrich had been banished to Siberia together with his wife and daughter Nesie. Already as a young girl she had to fell trees in a forest which were loaded on a sleigh and dragged to a river and unloaded on

Father's brother Heinrich and wife and their daughter Nesie and grandson Hans.

a frozen river. In spring, these were tied into a raft formation and floated downstream to the nearest timber mill. Later, Nesie told us that if she had not been able to pick so many wild berries to eat and can in summer, they would have perished due to hunger and malnourishment. Again, information flows both ways about parents, siblings and their families, with everyone reporting on matters that pertain to everyday life.

Father wrote not only in his capacity as a brother and brother in law, but also sent them a short meditation on the Word in every letter. He was thus able to serve them as a minister and custodian of the soul. His relatives much appreciated this service. Also, questions were raised. One of his nephews inquired about the form of baptism. This young fellow attended the service of the Mennonite Brethren or Baptists in Russia where only baptism by immersion is valid. Father answered him that forms of baptism are secondary to the faith with obedience to Jesus Christ being the primary concern.

Shortly before his death, father wrote his last letter to his children and grandchildren:

> By the time you will receive this letter I am long since at home with the Father of Light, with God, whom I was allowed to serve all my life long. In comparison to His light all the light of this world pales.
>
> My dear children and grandchildren, take care so that you will all arrive there. I long with all my heart that we will meet again in heavenly bliss. To that end walk the Path of Life, on which you have been placed by the grace of God. If you have an office to do for Him, or a service to perform in His Kingdom, execute it faithfully, be it big or small. Do not tire or grow weary, for God will honor His word, when He says, "I am with you till the end of this earth. And my strength is mighty in the weak and who asks, will receive. If temptations lurk, remain strong. Flee from the lusts of evil and keep your souls spotless.

Remember that the power of God will be yours if you will pray for it. If you should fall, do penance and flee to the cross of Jesus so that you will not lose your body and soul in eternity. Oh, my dear ones, I call out to you: Retain what has been entrusted unto you. Remain in what you have learned and remain, above all, in Jesus, our Lord and Savior. I am awaiting you in eternity.

CHAPTER VII

Father and Mother's Last Trip aka Final Journey

FATHER HAD A DIFFICULT time aging. He wanted to live long. There was so much of interest to him. The growth of the church but also the economic development of the colony fascinated him. When the fiftieth anniversary of Fernheim was celebrated in 1980, father and mother were in attendance. Together, with other pioneers of the settlement years, they sat in the front row during the celebration. When a Russian general addressed them in Russian, they were rendered speechless. They believed they still knew Russian but words now failed them. If one has not spoken a language for fifty years, one can still read and understand it, but speaking is a different matter, and the spoken word is not on the tip of the tongue any longer.

After father had given up as leader of the church, he still was involved but he had learned to say no if he was no longer up to the job of preaching. Mother came to his aid in simply stating that his preaching days were over. And so they learned to enjoy their retirement. Together they managed to visit their children and enjoy with them their farms or their occupations.

Mother found walking more and more difficult. Her knees were simply worn out from many years of work in the household and on the farm. When her children and grandchildren tried to help, she invariably said, "I can manage!" She greatly enjoyed traveling with father in their vw. Together they enjoyed the many trips to neighboring villages, or to Filadefia. Mother kept a sharp eye open for potholes, roving animals or other vehicles on the road. Father gently remarked that he was aware of all lurking dangers. Whenever father even put a slight pedal to the metal, she would gently remind him. Since a vw Combi is a bit high, mother had difficulty getting into it. This problem was easily resolved. She took a little foot bench along which she fastened to a thin rope and pulled into the van. Upon de-boarding, she released her little footstool by reverse tactic. She enjoyed it greatly when the two of them travelled together and they would not have exchanged the old Combi for the most beautiful Royal coach.

The morning service with our family had always been father's responsibility. When one of their sons, Helmut, dropped in one morning, the parents invited him to join them for breakfast. Then mother read the page from the Scripture Calendar with the footnoted Bible verses and then prayed from her good heart. Helmut had never experienced mother taking over the morning service. Since father had mounting difficulty in swallowing and his speech was also troubled, mother matter-of-factly simply took over the morning service. If one could not, the other took over; this was the story of their lives.

Father was completely involved in the building of the Old Folks Home in his neighborhood. He sacrificed the meadow of his own cows to that end. Our parents had no intentions of ever moving into this home. They intended to remain in their own home till death. When our older sister Liese visited them one evening, she found them seriously ill in bed. They were taken by ambulance to hospital where they recovered sufficiently to return home. The same doctor whom father had helped in the financing of his studies emphatically denied their insistence to stay at home. Uncle and Aunt Isaak now belonged in a Care Home. And that came to be.

This was a hard blow for father. He knew full well that the Care Home was the final station before the trip to an eternal home. Surely, he was not yet a candidate for the final journey. He fought another series of hard battles with his heavenly Lord and Savior. He knew from his earlier experiences that he would lose his last battle with God and it took him a while before he finally managed to say, "Thy Will, oh Lord, be done!"

However, he had two remaining wishes which God in His infinite mercy granted him. He wanted to experience the dedication of the new church. When that had indeed transpired, he wanted to experience the welcoming home of his son Hartmut, who was returning home with his family from Germany. On this occasion Dr. Dyck, with all his medical knowledge had to come to God's assistance to fulfill father's wish. They succeeded. Then father in

The fiftieth anniversary of Fernheim. The earliest church leaders Johan Schellenbergs, Jakob Isaaks and Gerhard Schartners occupy the front seats while a Russian general addresses the festive audience.

Photo of mother with her great, great grandchild Cristiano

Mother and father in the Personal Care Home and on their way, in 1980, to the consecration of their new church.

The new church in Filadelfia with the Old Folks Home located on the other side of the street.

A service in the new church.

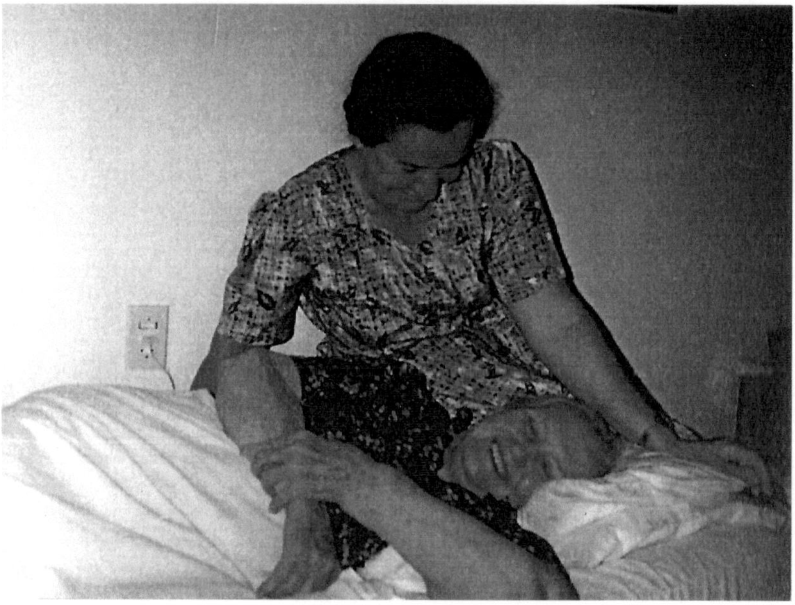

Mother and Elfriede have a good time.

mother's presence and some of his children as well, was able to peacefully fall asleep.

The stubborn, ambitious young man whose plans God time and again had destroyed until he became a pack donkey to his Lord, had finished the course of his life. The hostile Chaco bush which appeared to the stateless refugees from Russia as worse than a desert and which, after unspeakably hard labor and troubled care turned into the promised land of milk and honey for a large family, was his promised land. As incomprehensible as God's ways can often be, they could finally admit that, "The Lord first took from us all our earthly hopes to then give us an abundance of life in the disreputable Chaco. Praise the name of the Lord."

After the funeral mother stayed in Blumenort with her children on her old farm and then she was ready to move into the Old Folks Home. She lived there, surrounded by the love and care of her children and grandchildren for more than ten years.

In her diaries of those days she meticulously recorded daily temperatures and rainfall and everything else what had been decisive for the life of the Isaak family to date. She gladly accompanied her children to their homes and kept up a lively interest of their farming activities. On Sundays she always attended church services; the church lay opposite her home across the street. In her diary she frequently made accurate remarks regarding the ministers and their sermons. These could have been of service to them but mother would never have allowed airing of her observations.

When, however, her grandchildren occasionally expressed an overly critical opinion of a newly elected minister she corrected them by saying, "If this person is different from our expectations, we have to straighten him or her out through prayer."

Mother made reference to a most basic matter in saying this. If we intercede for a person before God, we do not change the person referred to. Only God can do that. However, if we intercede through prayer by an honest heart to God for a person, our own hearts are changed by that very act. The person in question again becomes a companion on the road to discipleship. We are then again in accord in helping others and help to bear a joint burden.

When mother celebrated her ninetieth birthday, all her children came home. For several days everything was as in former times when we sat together at the table and told stories about our lives. Then mother's face beamed like that of a bride. Whatever she had dreamt about as a young girl and then as a young mother had not been fulfilled. Instead of raising a large family on a rich Chutor, God had cast her into the wilderness of the Chaco. It was here that she had to prove God's wondrous guidance. When, during the early years, father had had such a difficult time in wrestling with God, it was she who provided the happy courage and great strength to lead, irrespective of situation; she invariably made the best of it. Without mother's selfless engagement and initiative, father would never have been able to develop into what he became and the large family would not have been able to grow up so carefree and

Mother in the care home.

healthy. It was particularly for her that the Word of God "Your faith will sustain you, and you will prevail!" applied.

When mother was more than ninety her strength ebbed. She still claimed "I can manage" but these words lacked conviction. One day she told one of her children, "This weary old hut of a body is falling apart bit by bit." As far as she was concerned, she was prepared for the old walls to collapse so that she could fall asleep in peace. Finally, God fulfilled her last and final wish. He called home this wonderfully gifted and blessed daughter.

As children, grandchildren and great grandchildren we can say that God gave us this wonderful mother, grandmother and great grandmother and when her time was up, He took her home. Praise be to His Holy Name!

The great inheritance which mother and father left us is the assurance that we will prevail if we believe in God's saving providence.

YOUR FAITH WILL SUSTAIN YOU,
AND YOU WILL PREVAIL.

ABOUT THE AUTHOR

HELMUT ISAAK was born August 5, 1939, in Filidelfia, the capital of the Paraguayan Chaco. After secondary and teachers' school training in Paraguay, he received a Licenciatura in Theology from the Mennonite Seminary in Montevideo, Uruguay (SEMT).

A generous grant from the Dutch Mennonite Conference (ADS) made it possible for Helmut to study Mennonitica at the University of Amsterdam where he obtained a Doctorandus in Theology.

Returning to Paraguay, Helmut taught for eight years at the Colegio de Loma Plata, Menno Colony, Paraguay, where he was also involved in environmental (creating parklands) and development projects (helping the Spanish Paraguayan neighbors set up their farms) in the neighborhood of the Colony, as well as working as youth leader with local Mennonite churches.

A second grant from the Dutch Mennonite Conference made it possible for Helmut to do post-graduate research in the Netherlands and in Northern Germany in 1977 and 1978, on the early development of the Anabaptist Reformation.

After moving to Canada in 1980, Helmut has served as senior pastor in four different churches as well as one church in Regensburg, Germany. Along with pastoral work, he has served as missionary in Mexico and Bolivia and he has given intense seminars on Anabaptist History and Theology in Santiago de Chile, in Bogota, Columbia and teaching at the Faculty of Theology of the Universidad Evangelica del Paraguay (CEMTA) for two and half years.

Helmut is the author of Menno Simons and the New Jerusalem which was published in 2006. He was instrumental in setting up the Anabaptist Peace Theology and Study Centre in (CETAP) in Asuncion, Paraguay, in 2006.

Helmut's academic and pastoral work continues to be carried out in multiple countries and cultures.

FSC
www.fsc.org
MIX
Papier aus verantwortungsvollen Quellen
Paper from responsible sources
FSC® C105338